half a look of cain

TRIQUARTERLY BOOKS
NORTHWESTERN UNIVERSITY PRESS

evanston, illinois

william goyen

half a
look of cain

a fantastical narrative

edited and with an afterword by reginald gibbons

TriQuarterly Books
Northwestern University Press
Evanston, Illinois 60208-4210

Brief portions of this novel appeared in *Mid-American Review* and
Southern Review.

The text of *Half a Look of Cain* and the materials quoted in the afterword are
published with the permission of the Harry Ransom Humanities Research
Center, University of Texas.

ISBN 0-8101-5031-X

Library of Congress Cataloging-in-Publication Data

Goyen, William.
    Half a look of Cain : a fantastical narrative / William Goyen ;
edited and with an afterword by Reginald Gibbons.
        p.   cm.
    ISBN 0-8101-5031-X
    I. Gibbons, Reginald.   II. Title.
PS3513.O97H33   1994
813'.54—dc20   94-13827
                                                                    CIP

The paper used in this publication meets the minimum requirements of the
American National Standard for Information Sciences—Permanence of Paper
for Printed Library Materials, ANSI Z39.48-1984.

contents

half a look of cain

"But why," I, the new Lighthouse Keeper, asked the Coast Guard Captain as we rode in the motorboat across the Sound to the Lighthouse, "did you allow this Curran to keep his post as Lighthouse Keeper if he was so very old and half blind?"

"We've been under criticism," the Captain answered me, "and perhaps justly, particularly as there was, in the treacherous fog that ended two days ago, a very terrible calamity: a ship carrying a little circus of animals and performers, coming up from San Francisco, crashed into the rock and the whole show was destroyed, so far as we can make out—but you have heard of it—drowned animals are still washing onto the shore, and bodies of the performers, too; although there has been no accounting, yet; and how can there be for some time, as the storm has just lifted and there is still disorder here. There may be survivors in the hills on the Canadian side."

"Yes, I've heard all this, just this morning," I nodded to the Captain.

"But you must know that this Curran had an uncanny genius for watching and seeing, in the pitchest darkness or through the most impenetrable fog; and his heroism, until the last, was miraculous. No one knew the waters as he, and no one we could find, even among our expert seamen, had the gift, the sense of boatsmanship in the rescue as Curran had."

"You scare me," I said, meekly. "I'm afraid I'll be a disappointment, coming after such a man." The Captain did not answer.

There was the Lighthouse, gray and strong; it was like a silo, a storehouse, in the wide calm field of water. The Captain was tying up the little boat at the lighthouse landing.

As we went up the winding ladder to the top of the tower, the Captain turned and spoke down to me.

"Don't be discouraged by the state of the tower. It looks about like the whole landscape today, as though the storm had broken into the room. As you've heard, he died a violent death, poor old Curran." And then the Captain looked at me very sternly and asked,

"You're sure you're not disturbed by the idea of murder? It may have been that, you know."

"But we are not sure it was murder," I said, "and it seems very likely, as you've said, that the old man went berserk in the storm, and particularly because of the shipwreck, and died in an agony of heart attack or brain hemorrhage. As he was so committed to his task, failure in it could have killed him. Doesn't that sound plausible?"

"He was like a god about it, yes," the Captain said, sadly. "He took it as a divine calling and mission. An extraordinary old man and one we shall mourn and miss."

When we entered the tower we found it as the Captain had said we would find it. The rescuers of Curran had literally done no more than to remove his body and close the door. They had found him sprawled among tattered and scrawled pages of writing; the winds of the storm might have blown them about the room, for the door was found open, and the spray of the great waves might have moiled what was written there, melting it all together.

"Here is where they found him," the Captain said, standing over a pile of ragged papers, "with the binoculars still in the grip of his left hand, as though they were a revolver."

"It was as though he had been killed by what he had seen," I said . . . "or by what he could not see . . . as though the instrument of his death was no gun or dagger, but a pair of binoculars." Now I saw that the walls were drawn and marked upon, but I could not tell what he had drawn or written there. The lines he had written were traced over and retraced until they were blurred as if one saw them through drunken or astigmatic eyes. And pinned on the wall by the window giving upon the long Strait that vanished out and up to Alaska and down and around to San Francisco, were three photographs which had been so touched and retouched that they were savage and monstrous shapes, more beastlike than human. I looked at one of them closely and saw that he had touched the lips and retouched them, the eyes, the cheek, so many scores of times, sometimes as if to reshape them, sometimes, it appeared, as if to destroy them, until it was like the face of a murdered man which still reflected the agony of violent death.

"I see that Curran wove," I remarked, pointing to a small loom across the room.

"He made pennants and flags for boats and ships," the Captain told me. "Too, it was something to do. The hours are long and lonely up here. You'll have to find something to occupy your free time, too. Maybe you can find an interest in weaving, as Curran did . . . unless you have some other interest."

"I've never tried weaving," I said, going over to the loom. "But I might try it." I looked at Curran's loom, and saw upon it the interrupted shape or design that he had been weaving. It was a careful shape, abstract and of no comprehensible image, so far as I could make out, except for the perfectly stitched shape of a human leg kicking the air and the body it belonged to submerged as if in water—or was it not yet woven in? I had felt, upon first looking at the figure on the loom, that its creation had been interrupted; but as I looked at it more steadily, I felt sure that it was finished. Running my finger over the fabric and down to the lower right-hand corner of the whole, I detected a little knot of Curran's thread and, without thinking, pulled at it. In a moment the knot, which was the bitter end of his long thread, seemed to snap back, as though it had been a stretched strand of rubber, recoiling with wild life in it through the intricate paths it had been drawn through to make this shape, until it reached the point where it had begun; and upon the loom and on the floor around it lay all the unraveling. I cried out to the Captain, across the room, "Oh my God, I've destroyed old Curran's long and careful work! Now what can I do?" I had the darkest feelings in me at that moment.

The Captain only looked over at the destruction I had caused— and added to all the other, almost as though I had deliberately wished to make it total—and said,

"The thread isn't harmed. You can use it all again, if you decide to weave. Maybe you can make even better shapes than old Curran managed to. Incidentally, somewhere in all this mess you'll probably find Curran's Log—and I imagine it will look like this room. But you might keep it as a guide for your own Log which you will, of course, begin to keep at once. After you've got an idea of Curran's Log, I'll pick it up and keep it—for the records."

The Captain and I worked for some time putting the room to order. At one moment, under a rampage of paper filled with scrawlings and drawn, inscrutable shapes, I found the Log, a typical large black book marked "Record." It was opened upon a page of clear, sure handwriting. I did not look at the recording but closed it at once and put it in the drawer of the desk by the window.

It was strange how I felt the presence of Curran, and it seemed a benevolent presence, not a haunted or morbid one at all, despite the word "murder" that hung over the room like a pall. It was a bright day, after the storm, and the Sound lay resting from violence. Something was over, after a long long time.

"His family were ferrymen for generations here on the Sound," the Captain told me, as he worked. "They've owned the only ferry-boat here all these years."

"Then he worked on the ferry," I asked, "before he took the Lighthouse?"

"Only as a boy," the Captain said. "When he became a young man of twenty or so he went away to study nursing, that was his real interest—not to be a doctor, but a nurse. He went abroad to study, to England, they say; and he was gone for many years. He did very great work there, it was told. When he came back, suddenly, to Port Angeles, he was a middle-aged man. That's when he took the Light-house, for he knew this country like the palm of his hand, and he's been here ever since, until . . . yesterday. As he was Irish—Port An-geles is predominantly Irish, you'll find; Curran's family were among the first settlers here, along with a few Finns—the town will no doubt have a big Wake beginning tonight. They'll bury Curran as a hero. His heroism in saving refugees from broken ships in storms on the dangerous reefs of the Strait is renowned. He could be seen in his little lifeboat, ferrying back and forth from shipwreck to Lighthouse; and many times the Lighthouse, high and clear of the torrent and the tempest, was filled with rescued travelers. He was a godly man."

After we had put the room to some order, the Captain left, bid-ding me good luck and begging me not to be too much disturbed, again, by the rumors of the murder of Curran. If I needed anything from shore, there was the signal light; and he, the Captain, would return in several days to see that I had got myself arranged for my new task. I said good-bye to him and thanked him for his help.

As it was darkening and the light over the Strait was failing quickly, I turned on the light in the tower and sat down to see how I really felt about it all. I saw through the windows the beginning fires of Curran's Wake lighting the shore, and before I was aware of it, he was so much in my mind and in the tower, I had taken the Log from the drawer where I had put it and began to read it.

I read all that night, looking up from the record to watch, through the binoculars, if ships were passing or approaching: but there were only little fishing boats passing or crossing, twinkling their icy lights, the steady crossing and recrossing of the ferryboat flying Curran's woven flag and crawling like a glowworm through the mysterious night, and the fires and keening voices of the Wake rising and falling from the shore. At daybreak I had read the whole story in the Log; and shortly thereafter I began my long duty in the tower of the Lighthouse.

I began, slowly, to copy down in my own hand Curran's Record, clarifying where I could the tragic and imperishable idea in whose service Curran exhausted his life. I had to have the Record for myself, and in my own hand. It is my copy which you read, coming to you from Curran through me—feeling as I do that we must put our hand on what is left to us, in this kind of collaboration, if we care enough about the ideas from which we are descended, like kin; and hoping to enlighten, for our own descendants, what was found in fragment and in half-darkness.

There is an idea running through this Record, like the running of the tide in the Strait, in and out, which might be dangerous if fallen into the wrong heads. At first this idea stole into my own head as calmly and as softly as a cat into the shade. But as the idea progressed I saw that it had the ferocity and the danger of a beast in it. I have seen in this second the manifest struggle of a man with an idea which infected him, and more: a personal heroism in the service of the idea, the uses of compassion and endurance and personal allegiance to an image which possessed him. I do not, I might interject, think the idea failed or betrayed Curran, though he was, it seems to me his copyist, the *victim* of it. You must judge for yourself, when you have read it. I know that the idea was not murdered, for it has infected me; and it is just that seizure of me by the expressed idea, if partially and fragmentarily and in the manner of fantastic notions (though, I feel sure, based on real experiences in Curran's own life), which moved me to record the Record.

It is, finally, I believe, a commentary on a man's time, and I feel that it might be of some use, of some enlightenment or amusement to those who read it, although many readers may be offended by or tire of the aspects of what they might see as allegory or parable in it. I have tried to leave the Record as it was when I found it, yet I may have become, in the copying of it, so enchanted with the idea in it that I could not know where my hand touched Curran's, seeming as it did to me, vaguely at first but more and more surely as I went on with it, that I had had the idea once, myself, and so claimed it in collaboration. And it might seem the same to you if you should be moved to record it in your own hand from mine. In this way we all join hands.

The Nurse's Record

To remind you of love, halt within us and waiting to be mended, that Beginningness that lies waiting in us all, I have to tell the story of a man of marvels, Marvello is his name; and to speak of beginning together: how the meeting and coming together of two human beings is a rescue; and how lovelessness is a perishing. To remind you of love and to recall to you its history, I speak all this, if you will listen to me, this tale that lives within my senses as if it were an odor smelled or the feel of a hand, the echo of a voice.

Now I speak at the end of a long time, and as someone very old, for I am an old man sitting in the tower of a lighthouse . . . it all comes to this, in the end, one voice in one small place telling what happened in many places and at many times in the broad world. The town is named Port Angeles, in the state of Washington, where I have come home, and it is a little town on the Strait: a landing-town where the ferry that crosses the Sound has stopped for many years. It will take you just the heart of one night to read what took so long to shape. I have got it all straight and simple by thinking about it many many years. I am an old man although I can still hear the flipping of a mullet and I can see out the window to pick out a famil-iar flag on a far ship; and I can cook my supper for myself: usually a little beans and broth.

My body is vanished, almost, so how shall I describe myself to you—I am no more than a little shrug of bones and hair. I feel as though I were only eye and ear and breath, and I speak of what I have seen and heard: my eyes and ears are in my mouth that tells: I have died and gone away elsewhere—and that, as I am now so far away from it, is what I am to speak of: *elsewhere.* In my face, if you could see it, you would find all the tracks of thoughts—deep ruts where they have, being sometime heavy like a loaded wagon, borne down their wheels deep into my flesh, and wheelshapes where they have spun around within their spoked prisons of themselves. You would find places in my face where thoughts have quarreled with themselves and struggled, disturbing the flesh; graves of pain and gravestones of hope that ended in grief; little pennants of joy; craters of sorrow; and a wide bountiful field of my blisses. You would see, if you looked closely, a cross for suffering the deaths of people who have died, upon my brow, a scar upon my forehead—from a fall. It is, then, this tracked and populated face, the landscape of my life: look at it like a map and you will discover the countries where I have lived. In one of these countries lived and will live until this face is covered with dirt, and then some, a man named Marvello, and what I am going to tell you is about Marvello.

Love, then, is the marrow of my story . . . I speak in language of the bone, which, it is said and I know well, is as slow to mend as the heart. So consider my voice the voice of a Nurse, a witness and servant to healing and repair. That has been my lifelong job. Old nurses, superannuated and the healing out of their hands, take it to their mind and there nurse over again all that was wounded and needed help towards healing and see, later, so much more of the mending process and what was mended, than then. My name is Curran.

Now old minds take a crooked way, so let me. It is the old mind that shapes best, in the end, so let it get there in its tarrying, studying way, as an old man crosses the fields—he gets there, and ready to tell of every little long-lived thing he has seen. Young tellers, full of passion and of a restless tongue, go too quickly and too hotly, often passing over the beautiful quiet little signs of things that are always there, on their way, which an old traveler knows to look for.

In the days of the War there was in London a young man who was just beginning his practice as what the profession calls a Physiotherapist. He worked with broken and afflicted limbs. He knew the bone. This young American nurse had come to St. Bartholomew's Hospital in London to finish his special studies when the War broke out. As you will see, this young man was myself. As Bart's, that ancient mending place, was in the danger area of the city of London, the orthopaedic ward was removed fifty miles away to the little town of Verulam, which St. Augustine founded—and on the Channel—and housed in what was once a grand old country mansion. The house had many gables and tented roofs with vanes and finials and steeples crested with iron pennants and iron birds hovering over or lit on them; it was three stories high, each story full of wide rooms whose walls had been pulled down to make long wide wards; and the great house was crowned with a round turret jeweled with little precious windows. On the top of the turret was a thin fierce spire upon which the figure of a rearing and strutted cock rose in the wind as if to trouble the air.

On the second floor of this converted mansion was a big barny room so crammed with cots that the wounded who lay side by side upon them could touch each other. This ward was a delicate world where men, rescued from great damage and out of violence, were suspended from wooden frames by cords and wires, hanging on frail netlike looms that were hourly manipulated by shuttles and purchases to keep them mobile. It was a world of fragile weaving and knitting, the laid-out broken body of a broken army. After the slow retreat through water and cold and darkness, under fire, these frail males had joined each other, so silently and so alone, as before, in this long slow march back, towards regeneration. Here, in this rude room, this simple long room of cot and patient, there was going on the most delicate and careful and imperceptible knitting, the slow stitching of frail threads of bone, the minute work of marrow and blood, remaking life out of its own substance. Men who had staggered exhausted and crippled and through water to this high, removed place—we had rescued them out of a flood— observed their wound as something so much greater than themselves but something they could bear and something which had a life of its own, quite apart from their own process of life, from their own human fictions and fantasies. If you came suddenly to the door of this room, it might appear to you to be another kind of battlefield, with little white tents in rows and men half-billeted in them, for the damaged limbs had to be protected by rooflike coverings. And then, on second look, you would be sure that it was a room of quiet and delicate work, of weaving and stitching, as if some intricate lace were being woven on long rows of wooden looms, because the men were strung upon these wooden frames as if they were figures being woven on the threads of looms by the nurses who stood over them manipulating them.

At the end of the War the casualties were moved back up to London, to Bart's, but Verulam continued to be used as a hospital for the lamed and crippled. I stayed on there, to continue my work as an Orthopaedic Therapist. The ward changed; it had another populace. This time there were several children in it, all boys of course, for it was a male ward; and we had a variety of patients. But the life, the inner life, of the ward was the same.

Beginning in about September, it rains and rains and rains in England. It does not really stop until around March, and if it goes on, which sometimes happens, there is a flood in low places. It was a day of slow rain when Chris, the young American, was delivered to the ward. He had had severe damage to his right leg from a fall in Europe, in Rome; and he had managed to struggle back to London with his two companions, a young man and woman. When he arrived in London he found, at Bart's, that his leg would no longer be of any use to him unless he had an operation on the bone. Bart's sent him out to us at Verulam, and we performed the operation on his leg. Now it appears that I am going to tell the story of this Chris when I had promised you the tale of Marvello, but to tell of Marvello I have to speak of Chris. For have you ever known people about whom you cannot speak without speaking, too, of another at the same time, because the two exist together like halves of a whole, and one brings the other to mind and so tells the other's story? So for Chris and Marvello. Part of a whole had been cleft from the whole, and we on the ward were mending a whole together again. Something of the whole is in every part of the whole and its parts remind themselves of the whole they belong to. The whole heals and afflicts its parts. I speak in these terms, then, to remind you again of reconstruction.

On a day of slow rain this Chris was delivered to the ward. He was in the company of, or I should say supported by, this young man and woman, for they were helping him along, each holding him under an arm, both very handsome, the girl dark and darkeyed, the young man greeneyed and fair. It was his face that struck me when I first saw it, for it was of such a dark mysterious look; and yet it had in it some animal ferocity. These, I knew at once, were not ordinary people and not from this country. They were, you could tell it, strangers.

It was an awkward time to receive a patient, for it was recreation hour and all the ambulatory patients were on the floor, either on crutches or in wheelchairs; but this young man was badly in need of bed and care. His friends—or deliverers—left him in my care and disappeared after embracing him. Suddenly the fair young man came back and asked me when the operation on "my friend" would take place; and I looked on the schedule and told him tomorrow morning at nine. "The young lady and I will be here," he said, and left. So I had this stranger in my care, and so it all began.

"I am Curran," I said to him, "and if you will come with me I'll lead you to your place." We maundered through the traffic of recreation hour, the Wireless was booming with music, men were calling at each other, nurses were giggling and running about, patients with great white plaster legs or sitting in wheelchairs or hanging onto a crutch were playing billiards on the huge table in the center of the room. There was such a whirling traffic of runaway wheelchairs that Chris cowered against the wall for fear of being run down, and then I knew how wounded he was, for the deeply wounded are most vulnerable to the wounded and protect themselves from each other. I knew he was thinking how he was, already, one of this lame and confined company. We found his cot and Chris sat down on it. I asked him how his leg was, and I remember he said it was "glittering with pain." I knew that he had an idea, a conception of his injury.

At that moment Bobby broke loose from the circle of rushing wheelchair traffic round the billiards table and skidded his little wheelchair alongside the table. He leaped in one springing leap onto the billiards table and the cues went up at once all around the table, like spears in the air, as if to threaten him who was so dangerous. In another flash, Bobby, quite like a very young and skinny unfeathered bird, was hopping and bouncing about on the butts of his joints, which were like cypress knees, in the middle of the table. Cries of "Now Bobby! now Bobby! off, Bob!" went up from all the billiards players; and I had to go over, calling "Bobby! Bobby!" With one bolt Bobby was off again and into his wheelchair, and in another instant he was whirling away again, amok among the cots, skidding up to the strung and balanced patients terrified that they might be unhung. Cries of "Bobby! Bobby!" from all the beds and billiards players and nurses sounded again, as if from that many parents. A nurse was chasing him now, and when he caught him and threatened to take him back to his cot, which had four high sides to it like a little pen, Bobby burst into screams and tears and whirled away again. Chris turned to me as he sat on his cot and asked who Bobby was. "He's been here since he was born, this is his home. He won't last long," I told him. "That's why we humor him. He was born without legs and has a knot on his spine."

Now a nurse had put Bobby into his pen and Bobby's screams had settled to a low, unbroken mewling from his prison. Often one of the men on the floor would go over to the child and speak softly to him, reason with him or pacify him, but it was as though Bobby could not hear them, as though he were in another world and he knew what it was, and he could not hear what his friends who loved him were trying to say to him, for what could they say that would help him, anyway? I saw Chris hunch down onto his cot as if to hide away from this motherless, womanless, doomed child.

I fetched Chris his supper but he would not eat it. Now the ward had changed into something very quiet, as though the tides were over, and there had settled over it, recreation and supper being past, a kind of docility and a sadness, as upon the twilight sea: men fell to sleep or read or lay remembering or hoping or planning. Chris was still sitting on the side of his cot, in a kind of trance the way animals are when they are brought into a strange room: they wait to get their animal sense of the place. Chris was reluctant to commit himself fully to the ward; but I told him to get into bed for I had to prepare him for the operation tomorrow. Suddenly the lights went down, it was darkening time, and Chris lay very still in his cot. Then the voice of one of the nurses in the low light spoke out the evening prayer, "Lighten our darkness, we beseech Thee, O Lord; and by Thy great mercy defend us from all the perils and dangers of this night . . ." I saw that Chris's head was turned away towards the window that held the night like a dark ocean in its panes.

Now in the settled quietness the noises of the farther room became audible . . . a kind of profound stirring as though one heard it from depths. Then in the darkness a voice from one of the cots whispered across to Chris, *"America, where do you come from?"* But Chris did not answer. In a moment he asked me in a low lost voice, "Tell me what is in that other room?"

"The critically ill," I said. Then the terrible ordeal going on in the other room, the deep suffocating sounds, the low cries, sounded again. Now that the ward was quiet, the sounds of the other room made it a profound reality. There was one low, steady cry that kept sounding and sounding like the call of one frail bird in a deep woods. Chris was listening to it as though it were calling to him.

"Who is it?" he asked me.

"A man who fell from a roof and shattered his limbs. He is in very great pain. So you see, you are not so badly off. Now try to go to sleep, for I shall have to wake you several times during the night to prepare you."

Suddenly Bobby begin to cry, first it was a whimper, then catching sobs, then a wail that seemed to stab Chris. "Nurse! Nurse! I am falling!" A nurse came soft-footedly to him and whispered, "Shhh

Bobby! Shhh! . . . you are having a dream . . ." Bobby's cry soft-
ened to small sobs, and Chris rose to his elbow and watched the
nurse rub Bobby's back and quieten him and tuck him in again;
then he sank down again, thinking, I knew, of the Rome he had
fallen in and of *Europe that had wounded him*. In a moment I said to
him, "Bobby dreams, as many of the legless do, of his lost limbs and
that he is walking. His dream is that he is walking and in peril of
falling . . ." And then Chris fell asleep under the sedation I had
given him.

I sat watching him and thinking about him, the mystery of him.
And then, in the quietness, against the low moan from the next
room, the voice of little Lord Bottle, as we came to call him because
his habit was to call, too frequently, "Nurse, the bottle, the
bottle!"—he could not control his animal functions—pierced our
quiet, and disturbed Chris: *"And the Lord said unto Cain, where is Abel
thy brother? And he said, I know not: Am I my brother's keeper? And He said,
What has thou done? The voice of thy brother's blood crieth unto me from the
ground."*

Lord Bottle was our intrepid little preacher, the child of evangelist parents who had enchanted him with prayers and hymns with
which he plagued the ward until we could, by force, stop his mouth.
He went on: *"And now art thou cursed from the earth, which hath opened
her mouth to receive thy brother's blood from thy hand: When thou tillest the
ground, it shall not henceforth yield unto thee her strength; a fugitive and a
vagabond shalt thou be in the earth."* Would no nurse come to stop
him? I waited, fearing to leave Chris.

*"And Cain said unto the Lord, my punishment is greater than I can bear.
Behold, Thou has driven me out this day from the face of the earth: and
from Thy face shall I be hid; and I shall be a fugitive and a vagabond in the
earth; and it shall come to pass, that every one that findeth me shall slay me."*
The ward was stirring in its sleep, but no nurse seemed to be coming. They were all in the Critical Room, busy with the perishing
whose deep sighs of exhaustion were the moaning undertone of
Lord Bottle's long pronouncement. *"And the Lord said unto him, therefore whosoever slayeth Cain, vengeance shall be taken on him sevenfold. And
the Lord set a mark upon Cain, lest any finding him should kill him. And
Cain went out from the presence of the Lord, and dwelt in the land of . . ."*
and then mercifully and abruptly the mouth of Lord Bottle was hushed by the hand of a nurse who had finally got to him. "Bottle! bottle!" the little preacher called to the nurse who was with him now.

"Go to sleep, Chris," I said. "I will tell you about the little
preacher tomorrow; go to sleep"; and when I put my hand on his

breast to pacify him I felt him shuddering with quiet weeping and watched him, finally, fade away again into the sleep I had brought him to.

During the night I prepared him three times for the operation. Each time he woke in a kind of trance, turning to me to say a name I could not clearly hear, but once I clearly heard him whisper "Cain!"; and I knew it was the word the little preacher had put into his drugged brain to make a dream, the way dreams borrow to make their substance. Early in the morning he asked me where I lived and I told him in the little turret. He asked me what I saw from there and I said the whole far countryside. Could he sometime, when he was better, go up and look out at England from the turret? And I said yes, I will show it to you when you are able. Then who was his doctor? And I told him his doctor's name and that he had met him around midnight when he had come in to see about him.

"But did I talk to my doctor, then?" Chris asked me.

"You gave him a good and clear accounting of yourself," I said, "And the doctor promised you, when you asked him, that you would leave Verulam with a good strong leg." Chris fell to sleep again.

The next morning—a fair day, the rain had stopped—they performed the operation on Chris and brought him back around noon. I need to tell you that there was a very good chance that Chris might never have his leg again, he had so abused it after he had wounded it, either not caring or thinking he could heal himself, in time. He was a very depleted young man when he came into the hospital, for he and his companions had traveled all over Europe and he had fallen in the very middle of the journey; and because he was so used up by some further expenditure of energy which we did not know about but observed the signs of—some deep-lived anxiety, some deeply searching secret of his—he rose faintly from the anesthetic like a leaf turned ever so delicately by a slight breath and then sank into a dead coma of exhaustion, as though he had withdrawn from us all. The whole right half of his body was stricken— somehow the injury and the operation had now affected the other parts of his body, and we feared that he might die.

I was assigned to this body—for where was Chris?—that swooned before me for how long I do not remember; there seemed no accounting of days. We raised the little tent over him and laced him onto the apparatus we called "the loom." My job was to keep his body mobile. Each hour I worked with the still, spread-out body, beginning with the head that rolled like an infant's in the hands, then the breast and torso, limp as rope, the limber loins, and then the delicate, mending limb. All during those days I watched and worked over Chris, wondering, "Who can you be and what in the world has happened to you that you would will to remove yourself from the living world?"

His two friends had appeared again the morning of the operation and they had waited in the corridor of the ward until Chris was brought down from the operating room. When we had put Chris on his cot, the two were given permission to come in the ward and sit by his cot to wait for him to wake. I noticed at first that they seemed to be quarreling and that out of the quarrel they reached an agreement, a hostile agreement of some kind, to the effect that each refused to come in to Chris with the other and that each would come alone to him. They finished their quarrel with the words, like some terrible finality drawn over the whole situation—which of them the pronouncement came from I did not know—"If he dies, you helped kill him."

But when Chris came to, for those several minutes, the two were suddenly standing by his side as though the quarrel had meant nothing, and I saw Chris look at the young man and young woman with half a look of hatred and half a look of love and then pass on away into his death of sleep. There was something between these three. The friends had brought, this time, the few personal effects of Chris's and I took them for him. In a few minutes, they left. They did not ever appear again. They had delivered him here, to me, it seemed, and had vanished, leaving his few possessions with me. These consisted of a little packet of photographs of Venice, all that beautiful naked race of people standing along the rims and on the rooftops of buildings and palaces, upon spires and colonnades; a large photograph of the three companions standing in the ruins of Rome, and a picture of the three standing together before the David of Michelangelo in Florence, Chris in the center under the loins of David, the girl and boy on either side. One of them had written under the picture the words, *"I would not see thy new day, David. For thy wisdom is the wisdom of the subtle, and behind thy passion lies prudence. And naked thou will not go into the fire. Yea, go thou forth, and let me die . . . yet my heart yearns hot over thee, as over a tender quick child."* There were also letters, opened and unopened, and a little silver box with words inscribed: "On silver, on clocks, on flesh, on water." Inside was a delicate gold ring with three stones, two bits of burning ruby and a tiny sparkling diamond in the center. The only other thing was a hidebound notebook on whose pages I saw what must have been notes, ideas, what?—put down by Chris? I put all these objects under the little tent we had raised over the patient, but I put the ring on his finger. It moved me to see the little relics and tokens of his expatriated life close to him, all he possessed, apparently, in the Old World, against his wounded and sleeping body, in that physical intimacy one loves to keep with the few small objects one cherishes. Chris no longer lived in his body, I thought: it had been removed from him, or he from it, drawn up and away. Under his tent there was only the haven of the dreaming mind and memory and desire; the rest, bone and flesh, was in other hands. I had only the stricken body to work with . . . but soon there came into my charge all other.

He hung, before me, footlong, in a hurtling shape, his right leg extended and toes pointed, like a dancer, his left leg bent at the knee and foot turned outward, as though, falling, he had been caught in a net by me who nursed and manipulated his body to bring it to move again. Every hour I would manipulate the strings and wires by means of little wooden shuttles, and the body of the youth would hunch and fall as the loom gently creaked and his body made forced mechanical movements which it seemed to resist fiercely. What strange powerful *resisting* life was in this apparently resigned body before me?

It *was* as though he had fallen, this figure, and as though we had caught him, here in this hospital and on this ward for the crippled, in this net upon which we had him stretched and fastened. We have rescued him, to put him back together again, I thought. The damage of the fall I could tell, for I could measure that by what I saw and worked with. The rest, what he fell from, where he fell, the distance of the fall and the damage of *that*, I had to measure by what I could not see or the fallen fully tell. Yet it is just this mysterious and invisible record which really tells the tale. What is broken, shattered, we put back together again in this mending place; we assisted the knitting of the bone and the stitching of the tissue; this was a place of rehabilitation. The process, briefly, is to elevate and hold still the afflicted member and wait until it finds its reality and its function again. It must find, itself, what it has lost or been bereft of, and by its own means. So much for the crippled limbs of men. But this was a place of the mind, too; for the mind, unhalted, runs on or runs back, and does its piecing, its regeneration, too. The relation of limb to mind is interesting, for limbs can lead a man in one direction while his mind is going in another: a man seen going down the sidewalk or the street is going one way, where his good legs take him and his arms, as though they were oars, row him. But who knows where his mind is traveling? In this place, then, where the limbs were of no earthly use, there was the traveling of the mind. Consider the many crossings and recrossings of the little rescue boat of the mind, from one shore to another, landing at islands perilous and benevolent, met by people on the shore or by none upon the lonely wastes and beaches. Looking at all these little rescue boats of beds in my ward, you would have known who was the invisible Boatsman.

Though the body of my patient, Chris, traveled some ways when I forced it by means of the mechanical apparatus I controlled, its journey was a wooden, mindless, heartless one, like that of a wooden Image on wheels and pulled by ropes. My patient's propelling power was behind and above, unseen. He would not go where any wood or line led him, but where he *had* to go. You see already the dangers that I knew, who might be moving him where he was *not* going—the selfsame dangers that befall a man who tells a tale of someone. Now you begin to see the responsibilities of a nurse.

There is something dreadful among us, I thought as I worked my loom with Chris upon it, a figure over the city we live in, to remind us; a shape in the streets following us; a ghost in the room we sleep and eat in, to remind us . . . a creature within us that could murder or keep life. The comatose Chris, in his state of profound insensibility, was on my mind every minute. I soon became obsessed with him. The danger was to *identify* myself with him—a nurse must not, finally, *care*, who cares and does not care. During those days we went on such a long journey, he and I, through more countries than I can ever tell you, though I can tell you some, and this is my purpose, will you believe it. You may say, in the end, if you will follow me through to it, that I was a kind of sorcerer and that I used witchcraft; but you must judge, when I am through, what witchcraft I used.

As I wove Chris as though I were remaking him, this putting together into a hale unhalted whole again became for me the only reality. Everything else was unreal: I had no words, no eyes for, no responses to anything outside this place where he was, in my charge, and where I sat or stood beside him. My work with him became a work of love, the mark of a good nurse. During the work of love, I lost my sense of relationship to the world around me; this work was the only reality and it drew all things to it. I lived for and through the mysterious process going on within this reconstruction which began with me by being manual and mechanical, using only my hands and my professional knowledge, and grew to be a whole experience involving all of me—and what happened was this: something in *me* was restored, Chris was bringing together lost parts of me. There was this mysterious double action, this marvelous reciprocity, the way we human beings work upon each other. My daily responsibilities beyond this work fell into desuetude; my living-place in the turret was like a violent man's, since I was never there to keep it in order. Rooms seem to fall to pieces without a human being in them. My friendships were neglected. I would not leave Chris night nor day, except to rest for an hour in the Lounge; and then he and I would be joined, even there, in my dreaming, and our dialogue would go on uninterrupted. Other nurses criticized me, but the doctor praised me. It was, then, a love-work, this nursing. But as there are storytellers who will tell you that they never let themselves get into a story they tell, so there are nurses who will say they have never suffered their patient's pain or healed a part of themselves in the patient's healing—but find me them! There is the marriage of pain and pain, of healing and healing.

Once, on my way to the Lounge to sleep for an hour, I saw, at the turning of the corridor and at the head of the stairs beyond, what I was sure was the figure of Chris, dressed in white and holding a tiny white infant in a blanket. With him were an old old man and woman, countryfolk. They were all very quiet and somber, as in a vision, and I saw that the baby was dead and that the young man who held it was not Chris, of course, but an Interne delivering the dead infant to the morgue. He turned to me and asked me if I would go with him and the old people to the morgue. We went, and in the morgue we laid the cold little corpse out on a stone slab for the old ones to look at. They were its grandparents. "It would have had Cornelia's nose," the old woman said, as if she were relieved. They were not moved by this little death, but quarreled over the expense of burying the infant. Their daughter could not afford it, they could not, either—and why should they? They had brought it to us to see if we would take it. The Interne and I told them that the Hospital would bury it and the two old people turned and left. We stood, the Interne and I, together with the little homeless death in our charge.

When I returned to Chris, it was as though he knew about it all. It was in this way that the shape of my patient—regard the word— became the living object to which everything that happened was related. I am speaking of a connection, woven, as of threads and veins and vessels, through which human beings may communicate and tell each other everything. I am speaking of the traffic that moves through us as in tunnels under ruins, the traffic through us, below the river, under the sidewalk. And this connection was between his dreaming mind breeding the images, on one side, on the other side mine, the shaping mind, conscious, controlled—or struggling to be—and the traffic beyond the wall, below the river, beneath the sidewalk. That is what I speak of.

I have had a lot of patients in my time, and I have learned from all of them—something about myself—as I nursed them; many times, in the end, I saw that *I* was nursed back, brought back to something lost sight or sense of. But Chris was the best patient I ever had. Sometimes I sit here on sunny days and watch the lapping waters of the crested Sound and think how I have tended a number of beautiful people in my time, but . . . *remember Chris?* And I remember how I have died with some and have been brought back to life with others, but . . . *remember Chris?* Always, in the end, no matter how many patients I go over again and nurse back in my memory, it is the same, in the end . . . *remember Chris?* We are this way, and therefore, bound together. We brought each other back, and I wonder if he knows or will ever know it, to tell it? If he would one day find me again! or I see him, as I thought to have seen him this morning: suddenly at the landing I was sure I saw, through my binoculars, his shape walking off the Ferry onto this Strait, limping a little.

We were in the country of his head where, I imagine, some image and some vision had seared his brain. For as I rolled that head about in the palms of my hands it was like some hot planet where the eyes were two craters closed over with caps of blue ice (they were so cold); and as I clasped the stem of his neck with the palms of my hands to stroke and gently knead it, the veins swelled out, with the friction of my palms, in little purple ropes to show me that the blood was rising to my call. There was a voice beneath this burned and blasted country.

What patients say to themselves or murmur for all to hear in anesthetic dream or coma, nurses must put into their records—and I might say that, apart from my profession, what people say to themselves or hear said to them by another has always interested me to the point of prying. I cannot, for instance, compel myself to ignore the letters of friends available to me; I will read them if I can possibly manage, as soon as they are out of the room. I have an uncontrollable desire to know all I can about people. I am a kind of spy, though I do not, believe me, gossip. I can be trusted to keep secret what I find out about people, believe me. Not all nurses are this unpurchasable, however. One of the nurses on the ward—I will not mention any names—would pry into everything a patient had about him and tell about it all, in the Lounge or at table . . . and added a lot to his story, I am sure of that. There are some nurses who do not have any life beyond the mail their patients get. But this nurse was his own disenchanter, for he would swear he had a Bulgarian Count as a patient until the patient awoke and cried out in the best Bow-bell Cockney for water. I will not repeat what I see when I watch out of windows or through cracks or keyholes of doors—or go even farther than that.

What I am getting to is that once, while I was working the wounded leg of my patient, the hidebound notebook fell onto the floor. I picked it up, and, if you will forgive me, understanding me now as you do, looked in it. There were many pages of Chris's (I imagine) own handwriting, sometimes neat and rapid, sometimes tortuous and jumbled as though lamed ideas struggled down the page. Was it a diary or a journal or the beginning of a long story he had to tell? An idea ran through my patient, as an idea runs through all of us—we are molded and shaped around that image, if we are whole; and we dangle and fall apart around it if we cannot pull it together to its whole and make it cleave to its parts. The wounding—and the destruction—of the idea has crippled whole races: witness some civilizations which have stood up straight and exultant in the flourishing idea they have created, to proclaim it at the very moment of its disintegration. It is burned in public, it causes wandering and exile and unspeakable suffering; it goes *below*, it sinks and strengthens itself, and some time, in its natural time, it rises again. I am speaking of the choice an idea has to make, and of the inner progress—damage, withering, coming to green again—of the choices of the spirit.

I finished my manipulation, then I sat down to read the writing. It had a title:

the figure over the town

How an idea runs through everything one sees . . . these ruins, these races; and how it finds a sensual expression; how the sensual grows into or out of the spiritual Idea, hangs on the back of the spiritual Idea, dragging it to its knees; and the struggle, eternally, seems to be between these two; at one era or epoch it is the sensual which has overwhelmed the spiritual and one sees the glittering remains, where the spirit had become a corpse, or an invalid, a limp white shape feeding its vampire; the famine, the starvation where the spiritual, a fleshless skeleton, swaddled its bones in robes of gold. And at one or two times, that identification of one with the other, that fusion of the two, producing the serene, removed, rescued marvel of, for instance, the winged lion on the great shaft or flagstaff in the Piazza de San Marco in Venice.

I will explore my perilous and majestical struggle, and I will do it by taking it *home*, to my own common ground, within my own experience *there* and in the light of what has happened to me *elsewhere*. How to bring this to form? I would choose an image out of childhood to begin with. The idea would be to begin with a childhood image and grow it up, mature it; and I would find it among real, plain folk whose consciousness had not yet fallen into a style; and I would search for it, even, among the ruins of a society. I would meditate the quarriers, the plowers and the planters. Such meditation knows no factions, has or takes no sides in the natural cycle, favors no one season over the other, functions in droughts, in floods, in sunshines and blizzards, in green garden or dry desert, in ruin or rebuilding. *To begin with*, then, I will have to combat and oppose prevailing opinions and styles of opinions. I will quarry through all that and lift my shape of patterns loose and free from all those disturbing and troubling forces.

Finally, I will make this shaped idea a living descendant from life, as in families, so that its forbears, its lineage, might be clearly defined and shown to have produced, miraculously, this heritor. And I could only hope that what was made, this descendant, might fall into the right hands, for it would have to rest upon and within other hands, it would have to be told and told again, threatened and intimidated, if it had any worth; and it would seem to me that the hands it fell into would take upon themselves a great responsibility not to overembellish what I had put into them, not to wrench or force so as to make true where it did not seem to be of truth in and of itself, not to modify so as to aggrandize it.

I would choose to examine with passion and honesty, as much as I could find and put to use within myself, being what I am, the marvelous thing that happened in my town which brought into my head the whole idea.

What I thought for so long was my doom but, I know now, is my hope, and all ours, takes the shape—or took it long ago when it was first branded upon my brain—of a huddled figure of a man aloft a flagpole. It took me a long time to see this meaning, and by the way of so much error and blind stumbling through half the experience of my life and through, it seems, half a race of lovers who fell into or were drawn upon my path.

Now each man, an army unto himself, carries with him both the artillery to kill or the flag to raise to truce—human relations have seemed to me like one eternal battle—we fight with the mind, with the heart, and with the loins, fierce weapons, or we simply come upon a man where he is working quietly at his task in the fields and bring him down at his work—with one blow. We draw back astonished from him suddenly lying struck down; are accused, flee branded by the murder and are "protected" by the brand from murder or from revenge by other hands. Fugitive, we carry the sign upon our bodies and we wander over the face of the earth with our burden, which is to reconcile the passions of hate and love, and to understand the evil act. No one will slay us—which would be our relief. . . .

In the town of my beginning, I saw this masked figure sitting aloft. It was never explained to me by my elders, who were thrilled and disturbed by this figure, too, who this figure was, except that he was called Shipwreck Kelley and that the days and nights he sat aloft were counted on calendars in the kitchens of small houses and in the troubled mind. Shipwreck Kelley fed the fancy of an isolated small town of practical folk whose day's work was hard and real enough.

It was at the time of a War; and since the night this figure was pointed out to me from the roof of our little shed where my father sheltered grain and plowing and planting implements, his shape has never let me alone; and in many critical experiences of my life this shape has suddenly appeared before me, so that I have come to see that it is a dominating emblem of my life, as often a lost lover is, or the figure of a powerful parent, or the symbol of a Faith as the Scallop Shell was for so many, at one time, or the Cross.

It was in a time of a War I could not understand, being so very young, that my father came to me at darkening, in the beginning wintertime, and said, "Come with me to the Patch, Son, for I want to show you something." The Patch, which I often dream about, was a mysterious fenced-in plot of ground, about half an acre, where I never intruded. I often stood at the gate or at the fence and looked in through the hexagonal lenses of the chicken-wire and saw how strange this little territory was and wondered what it was for. There was the shed in it where implements and grain were stored, but nothing was ever planted nor any animal pastured here; nothing, not even grass or weed, grew here, it was just plain common ground. This late afternoon, just at the moment of darkening, my father took me into this little pasture and led me to the shed where he hoisted me up to the roof. He waited a moment while I looked around at all the world we lived in and had forgotten was so wide and housed so many in dwellings quite like ours. (Later, when my grandfather, my father's father, took me across the road and railroad tracks into the large pasture that was so great I had thought it, from a window of the house, the whole world, where a little circus had been set up as if by magic or by a dream of mine in the night before, and raised me up to sit on the broad back of a sleepy elephant, I saw the same sight and recalled not only the night I stood on the roof of the shed but also what I had seen from there, that haunting image, and thought I saw it again, this time on the lightning rod of our house . . . but no, it was that crowing cock that always stood there, eternally strutting out his breast and at the break of crowing.)

My father waited and when he saw I had steadied myself and was fixed on the sight he had brought me to see, he said, "Well, Son, what is that you see over there, by the Methodist Church?" I was speechless and could only gaze; and then I finally said to him, not moving, "Something is sitting on the flagpole on top of a building."

"It is just a man," my father said, "and his name is Shipwreck Kelley. He is going to sit up there for as long as he can stand it."

When we came in the house, I heard my father say to my mother, lightly, "I showed Son Shipwreck Kelley and I think it scared him a little." And I heard my mother say, "It seems a foolish stunt, and I think maybe children shouldn't see it."

All that night Shipwreck Kelley was on my mind. When it began raining in the very deepest night, I worried about him in the rain, and I went to my window and looked out to see if I could see him. When it lightened I could see that he was safe and dry under a little tent he had raised over himself and gathered around him. Later I had a terrible dream about him, that he was falling, falling, and when I called out in my nightmare of Shipwreck Kelley, my parents came to me and patted me back to sleep, not knowing that I would dream of him again.

He stayed and stayed up there, the flagpole sitter, hooded (why would he not show his face?), and when we were in town and walked under him, I would not look up as they told me to;

but once, when we stood across the street from the building where he was perched, I looked up and saw how high he was in the air and he waved down at me with his cap in his hand.

Everywhere there was the talk of the War, but where it was or what it was I did not know. It seemed only some huge appetite that craved all our sugar and begged from the town its goods, so that people seemed paled and impoverished by it, as though it were some sickness that infected them, and it made life gloomy, that was the word. One night we went into the town to watch them burn Old Man Gloom, a monstrous straw man with a sour turned-down look on his face and dressed even to the point of a hat—it was the Ku Klux Klan who lit him afire—and above, in the light of the flames, we saw Shipwreck Kelley waving his cap to us. He had been up eighteen days.

He kept staying up there. More and more the talk was about him, with the feeling of the War beneath all the talk. It seemed a scary and an evil time. People began to get restless about Shipwreck Kelley and to want him to come on down. "It seems *morbid*," I remember my mother saying. What at first had been a thrill and an excitement—the whole town was there every other day when the provisions basket was raised up to him, and the contributions were extravagant: fresh pies and cakes, fresh milk, little presents, and so forth—became an everyday sight, like spires on churches and weather vanes on houses; then he seemed ignored and forgotten by the town except for me, who kept a vigil with him and a constant watch on him, secretly. Then finally the town became so disturbed by him—for he seemed to be going on and on, he seemed, now, an intruder (who could feel unlooked at or unhovered over in his house with this figure over everything that happened below in it?—it was discovered that Shipwreck was spying on the town through binoculars!)—that towards the last there was an agitation in the town to bring him down and the City Council met to this end. There had been some events of irregularity in the town which had been laid to the general lawlessness and demoralizing effect of the War: some robberies, the disappearance of a young girl, Sarah Nichols, the beauty of the town; but it was said she ran away to find someone in the War; and one Negro was shot in the woods, which could have been the work of the Ku Klux Klan. The question at the City Council meeting was, "Who gave Shipwreck Kelley permission to go up there?" No one seemed to know; the merchants said it was not for advertising, or at least no one of them had arranged it, though after he was up, many of them tried to use him to advertise their products, Egg Lay or Red Goose Shoes or Have a Coke at Robbins Pharmacy—and why not? The Chamber of Commerce had not brought him, nor the Women's Club; maybe the Ku Klux had, to warn and tame the Negroes, who were especially in awe of Shipwreck Kelley; but the Ku Klux were as innocent as all others, they said. The pastor of the church was reminded of the time a bird had built a nest on the church steeple, a huge foreign bird, and had delighted all the congregation, as well as given him subject matter for several sermons; he told how the congregation came out on the grounds to adore the bird, which in time became suddenly savage and dived down to pluck the feathers from women's Sunday hats and was finally brought down by the Fire Department, which found the nest full of rats and mice, half-devoured, and no eggs at all . . . the subject of another series of sermons by the Pastor, drawing as he did his topics from real life.

As the flagpole sitter had come to be regarded as a defacement of the town landscape, an unsightly object, a tramp, like a transient bird, it was suggested that the Ku Klux build a fire in the square and ride round it on their horses and in their sheets, firing their guns into the air, the way they did in their public demonstrations against immorality; and to force Shipwreck down. Perhaps he was going to be a wartime suicide. If this failed, it was suggested that someone be sent up on a fireman's ladder to reason with Shipwreck. Now he was regarded as an enemy to the people of the town and more, as a *danger* to the town, and even more, as a kind of criminal, who had at first been so admired and respected for his courage, and so desired, even; for many had been intoxicated and infatuated with him, sending up love notes and photographs of themselves in the provisions basket, which Shipwreck had read, obviously, and had later sailed down in the form of the Cross—for anyone to pick up and read, on the ground to the embarrassment of this one and that. There were a number of local exposures.

The town had been ready for any kind of miracle or sensation, obviously, or just for something to be excited or outraged by. A fanatical religious group took Shipwreck Kelley as the Second Coming, the old man called Old Man Nay, who lived on the edge of the town in his boarded-up house and sat at one open window with his shotgun in his lap watching for the Devil, unnailed his door and appeared in the town to announce that he had seen a light playing around Shipwreck at night and that he was some phantom representative of the Devil and should be banished by a raising of the Cross; but it was explained by others that what he saw was St. Elmo's Fire, a natural phenomenon. Whatever was given a fantastical meaning by some was explained away by others as of natural cause, and what was right and who was to believe what? An Evangelist of the town who called himself "The Christian Jew" (he was not a Baptist) had, at the beginning, requested of Shipwreck Kelley, by a letter in the basket, the dropping of leaflets, a sample of which was pinned to the letter. The leaflet, printed in red ink, said across the top in huge letters: WARNING: YOU ARE IN GREAT DANGER! Below was a long message to sinners. If Shipwreck would drop these messages upon the town he would be aiding in the salvation of the wicked. "The Judgments of God are soon to be poured upon the Earth! Prepare to meet God before it is too late! Where will you spend Eternity? What can you do to be saved? How can we escape if we neglect so great salvation (Heb. 2:3)?" But there was no reply from Shipwreck, which was evidence enough for The Christian Jew to know that Shipwreck was on the Devil's side; and so he held some meetings at night in the square, under the shadow of the flagpole, with his little group passing out the leaflets. "Lower Cain!" he bellowed. "You Sinners standing on the street corner running a long tongue about your neighbors; you show-going, card-playing, jazz-dancing brothers, God love your soul, you are a tribe of sinners and you know it and God knows it, but He loves you and wants you to come into His tabernacle and give up your hearts that are laden with wickedness. If you look in the Bible, if you will turn to the book of Isaiah, you will find there about the fallen Angel, Lucifer was his name, and how his clothing was sewn of emeralds and sapphires, for he was very beautiful; but friends, my sin-loving friends, that didn't make no difference: 'How art thou fallen from Heaven, O Lucifer, son of the morning,' the Bible reads. And it says there that the Devil will walk amongst us and that the Devil will sit on the rooftops; and I tell you we must unite together to drive Satan from the top of the world. Listen to me and read my message, for I was the rottenest man in this world until I heard the voice of God in my ear. I drank, I ran with women, I sought after the thrills of the flesh . . . and I admonish you that the past scenes of earth *shall be remembered in Hell* . . ."

The old maid, Miss Hazel Bright, who had had one lover long ago and he, a cowboy named Rolfe Sanderson, had gone away and never returned, told that Shipwreck was Rolfe come back, and she wrote notes of poetic longing up to him which she put in the provisions basket. Everybody used Shipwreck Kelley for his own purpose, and so he, sitting away from it all, apparently serene and in his own dream and idea of himself, became the lost lover to the lovelorn, the saint to the seekers of salvation, the scapegoat of the guilty, the damned to the lost.

But the town went on tormenting him; they could not let him alone. They wished him to mean their own dream or hope or lost illusion or they wished him to be what destroyed hope or illusion: they wanted something to get their hands on, around the loins if he would love them, around the neck if he would not; they wanted something to avenge some dark misgiving in themselves or to take to their deepest bosom, into the farthest cave of themselves where they would take no other if he would come and have them for themselves alone. They could not leave him alone. They plagued him with love letters and when he would not acknowledge their professions of love, they wrote him messages of hate. They told him their secrets and when he would not show himself to be overwhelmed by their secrets, they accused him of keeping secrets of his own. They professed to love him, to be willing to follow him, leaving everything behind; but when he would not answer to come with him, they told him how they wished he would fall and knock his brains out. They could not make up their minds and they tried to destroy him who had made up his, whatever it was he had made his mind up to.

Merchants tormented him with proposals and offers—would he wear a Stetson hat all one day, tipping it and waving it to the people below; would he hold, if just for fifteen minutes every hour, a streamer with words on it proclaiming the goodness of their lightbread, or allow balloons, spelling out the name of something that ought to be bought, to be floated from the flagpole? Would he throw down Life Savers? Many a man, and most, would have done it, to give a simplified and easily understandable reason for what his behavior was about, pacifying the general observer with some reason for what was done, and broad in the public eye, and in the general observer's own terms (or the general observer would not have it); and so send the public attendant away undisturbed and easy, with the feeling that all the world was really just as he, cheating a little here, disguising a little there, everybody was, after all, alike, so where the pain, and why?

But Shipwreck Kelley gave no answer. Apparently he had nothing to sell, wanted to make no fortune, to play no jokes or tricks, apparently he wanted just to be let alone to do his job; but because he was so different, they would not let him alone until they could, by whatever means they could muster, make him undifferent and quite like themselves, or cause him, at least, to recognize them and pay *them* some attention. Apparently he was not camping up there for the fun of it, for if so why would he not let them all share in it, they would do that; or maybe he was there for the pure devilment of it, like a cat calm on a chimney top . . . or for some very crazy and not-to-be-tolerated reason of his own, which everyone tried to make out, hating secrets as people do who want everything in the clear—where they attack it and accuse it and take moral dudgeon against it.

Was it Cray McCreery up there—had somebody made him another bet? One time he had walked barefooted to the next town, eighteen miles, because of a lost bet; but no, Cray Mc-Creery was found, as usual, in the Domino Parlor. Had any crazy people escaped from the Asylum? They were counted and found to be all in, home. The mind reader, Madame Fritzie, was importuned: she could not find out one thing. There seemed, she said, to be a dark woman in the picture, and that was all she contributed, "I see a dark woman . . ."; and as she had admonished so many in the town with her recurrent vision of a dark woman, there was either an army of dark women tormenting the minds of men and women in the world, or only one, which was Madame Fritzie herself. She could have made a fortune out of the whole affair if she had had her wits about her to see the right things. More than one Ouija board was put questions to, but the answers were either indistinguishable or not to the point.

Dogs howled and bayed at night and sometimes in the afternoons; hens crowed; and the sudden death of children was laid to the evil power of Shipwreck Kelley over the town.

A masked buffoon came to a party dressed as Shipwreck Kelley, and for a while he caused increasing uneasiness among the guests until three of the men at the party decided to take subtle action rather than forcibly unmask the stranger, and reported the incident to the police on the telephone. The police told them to unmask him by force and they would be on their way. When the police arrived they found it had turned out to be just Marcus Peters, a practical joker with the biggest belly laugh in town and past president of the Lions Club, and everybody could have known all along that the impostor was he if he had only laughed.

A new little language evolved in the town: "You're crazy as Shipwreck"; "cold as a flagpole sitter's . . ."; "go sit on a flagpole"; and a high school girl riding home from a dance said to the football player whose lap she was sitting on, "What do you think I am, a flagpole sitter?"

In that day and time there was flourishing, and even in that little town, a group of sensitive and intellectual people, poets and artists and whatnot, who thought themselves quite mad and gay—and quite lost, too, though they would turn their lostness to a good thing. As these advanced people needed an object to hinge their loose and floating cause upon, they chose Shipwreck Kelley to attract attention to themselves, which they so craved. They exalted him to some high, esoteric meaning which they alone understood, and they developed a whole style of poetry, music, and painting, whose echoes are still heard, around his symbol. They wrote and read aloud to meetings of each other exegeses on and examinations upon the Theory of Aloftness.

Only Mrs. T. Trevor Sanderson was bored with it all, shambling restlessly, the way she walked about the hospital in her Japanese kimono, with her spotted hands, which meant liver trouble, the doctors said, spread like fat lizards on the knolls of her hips. She was there, again, for one of her rest cures because her oil-money worries so wore her to death, and now the Catholic Church was pursuing her with zeal to try to convert her—for her money, so she said. Still, there was something to the Catholic Church, you couldn't get around that, she said, turning over her spotted hands to show them yellow underneath like a lizard's belly; and gave a golden windowpane illustrating the Temptation of Saint Anthony to St. Mary's Church, but would not go farther than that.

There were so many little felonies and even big offenses of undetermined origin in the police records of the town, and Shipwreck was a stimulus to fresh inspection of unsolved crimes. He drew up to him, as though he attracted blame, the suspicions of the town, and he absorbed them like a filter, as though he might purify the town of its wickedness. If only he would send down some sign of response to what had gone up to him. But he would not budge; and now he no longer even waved down to the people below as he had during the first good days. Shipwreck Kelley had utterly withdrawn from everybody. What the town finally decided to do was to put a searchlight on him at night to keep watch on him.

What with the searchlight on the flagpole sitter, the whole

thing took a turn, as ideas do which seem for a while insupport-
able but, in another light, obsessive as they are, become an
excuse for a ribald attitude. The town began to be gay with
Shipwreck. When a little wartime Carnival came to the town, it
was invited to install itself in the square near the flagpole sitter,
and a Bazaar was added to it by the town. The spirit of Shipwreck had to be admired, it was admitted; for after a day and
night of shunning the gaiety and the mockery of it all, he showed
his good nature and his good sportsmanship—and even his
daring—by participating! He began to do what looked like ac-
robatic stunts above the town, as though he were an attraction
at the Carnival. But what would the people do, after a while,
again, but turn against him and say he was, as they had said at
first, a sensationalist? Still, I loved it that he had become active,
this *idea*. I loved it that *my* idea participated in the whole show,
that it was not a static, fastidious, precious, and Olympian idea,
that Shipwreck did not take on a self-righteous or pompous or
persecuted air about it all; although my secret conception of
him was a tragic one. I was proud that the idea fought back—
otherwise it was like Old Man Gloom: a shape of straw and
sawdust in man's clothing: let them burn him, gloom only stood
there, among the executioners, watching its own effigy and
blowing the flames. I see now that what I was watching was the
conflict of an idea with a society; and I am sure that the idea was
bred there by the society, raised up there, even, by the society
that opposed it, and not removed from it; in short, that society
was in the flagpole sitter and he was in the society of the town.
But the difference was that the flagpole sitter was thinking in
terms of the community, I believe, while the town was thinking
only in terms of itself.

There was the little carnival around him. One concession
called "Ring Shipwreck's Bell" invited customers to try to strike
a bell at the top of a tall pole resembling Shipwreck's and with a
replica of him on top by hitting a little platform with a rubber-
headed sledge hammer. There were other concessions where
people could throw darts at a target resembling a figure on a
pole. The Ferris Wheel was put up so close to Shipwreck that
when its passengers reached the top for a magical instant they
could almost reach over and touch his body. Going round and
round, it was as if one were soaring and rising up to him only to
fall away, down, from him; to have him and to lose him; and it
was all felt in a marvelous and whirling sensation in the stomach
which made this experience the most vaunted one of the show.

This must have tantalized Shipwreck and it must have seemed to him that all the beautiful and desirable people in the world rose and fell around him, to give themselves to him only to withdraw from him untaken and ungiven, in a flashing wheel of faces, eyes and lips and tongues stuck out to him and sometimes a thigh shown him or a hand offering a breast or sex, and then burning away, like the temptation of Saint Anthony. His sky at night was filled with voluptuous images of flesh and desire, and often he must have imagined he saw the faces of those he had once loved and possessed turning round and round his head to torment him. But there were men on the wheel who made profane signs to him and women who stuck out their rumps at him, fingering their noses. Soon he raised his tent again and obscured himself from his tormentors and the tormented. But what specifically caused this withdrawal was the attempt of a drunken young man to shoot Shipwreck. This young man named Maury rode a motorcycle around the town at all hours and loved the mean streets of the town and the good women who gave him ease on them, especially the fat ones, his mania. One night he stood at the window of the hotel and watched the figure on the pole that seemed to flash on and off, real and then unreal, with the light of the electric sign beneath the building. He took deep drags of his cigarette and blew the smoke out the window towards Shipwreck; then he blew smoke rings as if to lasso Shipwreck with them, or as if his figure were a pin he could hoop with rings of smoke. "You silly bastard, did you like what you saw?" he had muttered, "Where have I seen you before?" between his half-clenched teeth, the way he spoke that made him so seductive to people, and fired. Shipwreck turned away, once and for all. But he had not turned away from me.

With all this in my mind, I the silent observer, watching from my window or from any high place I could secretly climb to, witnessed the conflict of sides and the tumult of the town. One night in my dreaming of Shipwreck Kelley—it happened every night, this dream, and in the afternoons when I had to take my nap, and it had gone on so long, this dreaming of him, that it seemed, finally, that he and I were friends and that we met in the rendezvous of my dream where he had come down secretly to me in the little pasture (years later I would know what all our conversations were about, but not for many years and after so much—he lived, alive and real in my room where the dreaming of him happened, he was the only one in the world who knew me)—that night in my dream the people of the town came to me and said, "Son, we have chosen you to go up the flagpole to Shipwreck Kelley and tell him to come down." In my dream they led me, with cheers and honors, to the top of the building and stood below while I shinnied up the pole. Shipwreck's tent was up, for it was raining in my dream; but a great black bird was circling over the tent. As I went up the pole I noticed crowded avenues of ants coming and going. And when I went into the tent, I found him gone. The tent was as if a tornado had struck inside it and wrecked the whole world of it; there were piles of rotten food—he had not eaten any of the provisions they had sent up—shreds of letters torn and retorn a score of times, as small as flakes of snow; photographs pinned to the walls of the tent were marked and scrawled over until they looked like photographs of fiends and monsters; corpses and drifts of feathers of dead birds that had flown, in their night flights, into the tent and gone so wild with fright that they had beaten themselves to death against the sides of the tent. There was a floor of feathers and decaying food and the litter of torn letters. And over it all was the vicious traffic of insects that had found the remains in the way they sense what human beings have left and come from miles away to get it. What would I tell them below who were now crying up to me, "What does he say, what does Shipwreck Kelley say, Son?" and there were whistles and Indian calls and an increasingly thunderous chant of *"Bring him down!* Bring him down! Bring him down!" What would I tell them? I was glad he had gone; but I would not tell them that, yet. In the tent I found one little thing that was not touched or changed by Shipwreck: a piece of paper with printed words in red ink and across the top the huge red words: WARNING: YOU ARE IN GREAT DANGER!

Then, in my dream, I went to the flap of the tent and stuck out my head. There was a searchlight upon me through which a delicate curtain of light rain fell; and through the lighted curtain of rain that made the people seem to be far far below under shimmering and jeweled veils, I shouted down upon all the faces of the multitude which was dead quiet, now, "He is not here! Shipwreck Kelley is not here!"

There was no sound below from the crowd who did not, at first, hear what I said. They waited, then one voice bellowed up, "Tell him to come down!" to make me say again what they would not yet believe; and others joined this voice until, again, the crowd roared, "Tell him that we will not harm him; only tell him he has to come down!" Then I waved down at them to be quiet, in the gesture of Shipwreck Kelley's salute as he had waved down at people on the sidewalks and street. They hushed to hear me again. Again I said, this time in a voice that was not mine but in my dream it sounded large and round and resounding, "Shipwreck Kelley is not here, his place is empty."

And then, in my magnificent dream, I closed the flap of the tent and settled down to make Shipwreck Kelley's place my own, to drive out the insects, to erase the obliterating marks on the photographs, and to piece together, with infinite and patient care, the fragments of the letters to see what they told. It would take me a very long time, this putting together again what had been broken into pieces and by so many lovers and killers; but I would have a very long time to give to it, and I was at the source of the mystery, removed and secure from the chaos of the world below that could not seem to make up its mind and tried to keep me from making up my own.

My dream ended here, or was broken, by the hand of my mother shaking me to morning; and when I went to eat breakfast in the kitchen I heard them saying that Shipwreck Kelley had signaled that he wanted to come down early that morning, around six o'clock—he had come down in his own time—and that he had come down very very tired, having set a world record of forty days and nights, the length of the Flood. I did not tell my dream, for I had no power of telling; but I knew that I had a story to one day shape around the marvel and mystery that ended in a dream and began in the world that was to be mine.

There are some dreams or images or visions that we had better not pursue too fervently unless we are prepared to face what knowledge, terrible or beautiful, they might, finally explored and opened out fully, reveal to us . . . (Now, my patient, I thought, looking up from his written words to his sleeping face, what are you leading me into that I might not want to know? Yet he had already led me so far that I could not turn back, in this silent conversation he and I were having. I turned back to the notebook.)

Yet if we kill the dream or the vision, there is the phantom of that assassination which follows us through all our fugitive days. This seems to me, briefly and simply, the human plight and man's eternal conflict. But there is nothing to do but face what we dream or kill it and run away, bearing upon our spirit and often upon our face the mark of the murder.

For a while, as I grew, I loved my dream of Shipwreck Kelley and held it close to me like another body in my bed or stayed close to its shadow all day long as though it were my beloved companion beside me. I did not bother its meaning yet; I only

saw that it seemed to mean, this dream, everything I saw and felt, the dream lived in my *senses*, as lovers do and as all beautiful things do, in the beginning. But when I turned my mind to the dream, another thing happened. I was led away.

I looked up again and said to Chris, "*You are leading me away, my patient; and wonder should I go?*" What would you have done? After all, I said to myself, I am only trying to get a better sense of my patient—and so of course I read on. I began to *tend the notebook:* I had two lives in my care, one struggling to die, one to come alive. Already, it seemed that *I* had to make a choice as to which to keep. I found a fable, and put it down:

The Fallen Aerialist: Marvello's Story

(CURRAN'S FABLE)

"Thou seest this man's fall, thou seest not his wrestling."

I was twenty when I followed away from my town a trapeze family, aerialists, a group of beautiful winged people, mother, father, son and daughter. They were the Ishbels. Their flights and falls bewitched me; my ambition was to join this family. I followed the circus away, and I did not even say good-bye to my mother who was ill and lay all the time in bed, now; or to my father who was a silent, sad man, and why? I felt I was stealing away, as if I were turned out for a crime I could not name but felt a secret guilt for . . . this sense of belonging to dangerous and double things, being claimed by them. For in those perilous days there at home and in that town, it was, I saw later, the problem of learning how to use my sensibility, how to keep from perishing from it. Often I thought I would die through my senses. I was, I discovered, extraordinarily equipped for love, being endowed with those sensual properties that set men wild in some hunt. The French have a name for such a young man who cannot stay still: *cerveau brûlé:* "burned brains." I had a fire in my brains. Alone around the place, my home, that seemed to be dying, I went about in my hot secrecy and my goading loneliness with my desire that made me speechless when it possessed me as though it burned my tongue out of my mouth, and seared my words away. I fell into fits of speechless trembling, and I did not know how to use it, my desire. I sensed that it was meant to set something in motion, some beautiful flight or fall, and to finally erect some permanent structure. I felt, in that vague way of youth, that it was to be turned to greater use than combustion of flesh and that it was not to be consumed only sensually, that was not enough, there was a further use. Yet this was the danger of my age where men burnt themselves out in sensation and where the sensational was the celebrated and the glorified. I had to learn this, and that is the world whose style I ran away into, fell into, and was almost destroyed by before I made the choice. My desire, I felt vaguely, was not, then, to be consumed only sensually, but it might, like a furnace, produce power to turn something to light or to heat, through some *work*. It was a *natural* desire, then, after the ways and works of nature. The style of my time, I found, was unnatural or supernatural or preternatural, against nature; and I was an instrument of nature—can you already see my danger? But what I had to do was to learn the evil uses of my desire, its destructive uses, and this I did in ways I cannot tell you now, it is not the time or place, we are not yet in that country. I wormed and kicked, strangling in the ashes of my most magnificent fires; and I bruised myself against the burnt-out clinkers of those I had depleted in the hot uses of my desire. Yet who of us has not done this? It is time to tell. I lay with any body, a whole race of imagined beautiful people, to heal a throbbing pain; yet what was healed?

I followed the circus and worked at menial jobs with it for which I was not suited; but I was waiting. In time I made known my ambition to be an aerialist, and in time the Ishbels made me an apprentice to their son, Pietro. Ishbel, the father and husband and Master, trained me every day. I began my training by sitting at various levels of height for gradually increasing lengths of time until, finally, I was at the very top of the tent, sitting there for an hour—this was to adapt me to the sense of being *over* the wide mass of humanity below that would watch and ultimately acclaim me, to condition me to the solitude of height and to arrange me to air. Ishbel was a magnificent man of nature; his sparkling waters and gleaming fires, a shape of crystal breath in cold light is the only way I can describe him, for, again, he was described by the senses the way an odor or a sight or sound is given shape by nose and eye and ear, beyond words. He was more like a gentle beast than human. Yet in his face, round as an

Earth, was all humanity. Sometimes I thought, during my apprenticeship, that it would be enough to work with him in an Act of two, that we might together, abandoning the family, form a splendid Act that would shake and turn the world in another direction; but no, it was the family I wanted to join, to be in the air with. Sometimes as I sat at my new height I would be filled with fears, looking down upon the round Earth face of Ishbel below, and the fear of falling chilled me. Then I would cry down, "Ishbel! Ishbel! I am falling falling!" Ishbel would call up to me, "If you fall, I fall!" We had this kind of relationship. We worked within a secret rapport, undefinable, so ask no name for it . . . and if you need a name, call it the arrangement of air.

The time came when I was ready to join the Family. It was a sold-out show that night, in San Francisco. In the family tent where we were quietly waiting for the trumpet to announce our appearance, I thought, suddenly, how I or any one of us could destroy the family, and in that moment I was appalled at the thought that I might be moved by some demonic will in me to destroy the Act of the family. After all, I was only an adopted member of this family, our blood was different. Nothing could change that. But the trumpet sounded, and we sprang and danced out into the ring. The Act began. Ishbel, the splendid-bodied animal, stood in the center of the ring and flung each of us up into the air to the lower hanging bars, first his wife, Isabella, then his daughter, Marabella, then the son, Pietro, then me, the adopted one. I flew up like a bird, hearing, as I soared up, the words of Ishbel whispered to me, "Remember if you fall, I fall . . ." Now we were all on our levels, and in one moment we were in our flights, rising higher and higher, in the glittering lights. Once, in my dizzying winnowings and dartings, as though I were, now, a fish in this smooth water of air, I slipped and fell some little distance into the arms of Ishbel; but in a flash I was free of him, in control of myself again, as though strengthened by Ishbel's touch, and the crowd below never noticed the slip. I saw the flecked nets below us like foam of an ocean; but already I saw that now I was flying like a bird from the boughs of the family: I used them, now as a bird a tree, to climb higher and higher; and I perched, ultimately, like a stunning ornament at the very top. To make one's beginning with very beautiful and rare people is dangerous; but we were a dazzling success that first night, and I was saluted by the crowd at the end of the performance as the glory of the act, the very darling of the family.

So I had become, at once, the star of the family, and my renown spread worldwide overnight. It seemed that the Ishbel Family Act existed only to display *me,* and they were certainly the first to agree with the world that I was a marvel to behold. They named me Marvello.

We went from city to city and I was the Prince of each. But something began to happen in me: my life became disordered and I felt bent on some kind of destruction in the world outside The Ishbel Act. Something left over from the work of the Act or something generated by the work of it—what?—brought this changing within me. At night, after the performance, I would go into the cities we played in and hunt. Since my body was craved by hundreds of anonymous people in the audience, I was no stranger in the town. I gave it willingly to whomever wished it and if they were beautiful and if I wanted them. My only requirement was that we wanted each other. I found and knew all ways of love, and my lovers flocked after me and followed the show sometimes, from city to city. My body's hungers were insatiable. My life seemed basic: the only thing in it, the very center of it, was The Ishbel Act; and whatever I indulged in beyond the Act seemed passionately related to it. Sensual love seemed to enhance my genius in the air and to so beautify my work that my achievement became more dazzling than ever. The Ishbel Act itself began to take on a sense of my own wild life and strived, as a whole, to become more daring. But I excelled them and seemed to tarnish what had once shone, without me, or to have stolen their brilliance. I did not question the connection, the relation between air and ground, between what I created above and what I destroyed below.

But then a change began, as within me, within the world that loved and celebrated and watched me in my work. They began to say that I corrupted the young. Parents feared me and would not bring their sons and daughters to watch me perform. Sons and daughters came anyway, secretly or in defiance of their parents. I became a kind of Cause. I influenced many to leave home and to begin a sensual life of their own. Some of them, who had the genius for it, found great success and achievement. Others, who had nothing more than a lust for imitating, were destroyed, on the ground. (But had I misled *these?*)

I caused a kind of revolution among the young. They would come to me and say, "We need you, Marvello, you must speak for us!" Towns forbade me to perform, committees drew up interdictions against me and citizens signed them, and sometimes there were armed authorities at the gates to the tent to keep out the young. But then I disturbed the older and the old, who were not invulnerable to me; and so what was there to do? Despite the laws and acts of prohibition, the proclamations against me, the riots outside the tent, I went on, smuggled into the ring so mysteriously that my marvelous Act was enhanced by the very opposition that tried to destroy me; they could not catch me. They could do nothing to restrain me once I was in the air and above them all, there was no way to bring me down. Then they were so transformed and enchanted that they could do nothing but watch, in the kind of sensual trance I caused in them. And so I dazzled them again; and so my act became an act of exceeding danger. By this time, the Ishbels were no more than the machinery to hoist me into air.

I began to consider my great and beautiful power. What was the machinery in me that roused such responses and turned so many hearts? Was it for good or for evil? I was not an evil man, I thought. If I were to raise up, suddenly, a Cross, or to hold out the Bleeding Heart as the images in churches do, as I perched, in that blinding moment of the apotheosis of my Act when I lit, in a shimmering mist of light at the very peak of the tent, the very top of the world within the tent which I had created—the most delicate, sparkling world of glittering fires and ices—how many would I turn to the Cross and how many would I lead to its cause of charity and mercy and so change, in great part, the course of men who had seen me? My own power, which seemed to come from somewhere beyond me and through me to others, baffled me, for it had love and evil in it, both life and murder, hope and doom. But I would not quarrel with it or analyze it beyond the recognition of it. Yet the recognition of it was my first step toward the very destruction of what I considered and recognized: I was at a dangerous crossing. Those who spoke to me or wrote to me or lay with me told me that at that apocalyptic moment of my Act of which I have spoken, I resembled the shape of the instrument of love, and that this was the shape that was burned on their brains and became their memory of me when they were alone in their beds or walking in the streets, and led them to the acts which I was accused of provoking in them. This astonished me, but I would not ponder it. I roused a generation of Burned Brains, they left lovers and homes and friends, restless and seeking, and I came to know, now, that I was that dangerous leader of men who treads the edge of the abyss of hellfire, who could influence to good or evil. I could not turn back. Knowing what I knew, I could never forget my knowledge of my own powers; and whatever door I opened to flee my fiery room where I stood, flaming among the flames, opened again onto the same burning room. I was the man who could not choose but who had to make the choice, every day, every night, between love and death, life and murder. I was against the style of my time.

They accused me of witchcraft. But I had thought I was only searching for my own reality, regardless of the consequences, in a time when men could not find theirs. My enemies were countless and they, as I have told you, were out to bring me down, to destroy my power and my influence, my act. The tent, during my Act (the Ishbels now only stood on the ground beneath me like statues) became a battleground, a theater of war; it became a secret stolen place, a rendezvous for the fantasies of the lonely and the love-hungry and the abused who were the victims of their own human race; a *front* for the cause-hunters who would try to misuse me and my power to their own ends. Each man and woman felt himself to be alone with me, just the two of us, in a hidden tower of voluptuousness, and such a wave of sensuality came over the world of the tent that it seemed to burn with desire and longing.

But if my accusers and my enemies were inimical to my Act, my defenders were killers. These would come to me as if they had made me and say, "We want to give you a prize"; or "I am Chairman of the Committee of Awards and Honors of this city. We have decided that if you change your Act, a bit here, a bit there, then the audience will acclaim you and your enemies will accept you and the Committee will then be honored to award you the highest prize it offers. Otherwise, we shall have to give the honor to Benuto." And when I asked who was Benuto, the Chairman informed me, "He has won great recognition for his Act, inspired by you and obviously influenced by you, but he has been willing to make the slight change necessary to bring to it that wide acclaim and applause which you lose to your enemies."

So my Act was being imitated over the country, in Night Clubs and Carnivals. Imitators were brought or came to me—little dolly-faced performers who, disguised as Kewpies in their act, leaped through burning hoops and were never once singed; and big-haunched, slow-lipped women from The South; and those who talked a brilliant Act. I could see that they had debased to success what I had found in my own nature, by pretending that it rose out of theirs, too; and a whole style of aerialism developed that was loathsome to me, for it was a betrayal and it was easy; they would never fall, they did it with nets and mirrors. They were trying to bring me to conform to this style, a safe, facile imitation of myself! They threatened extradition and exile if I should not.

But the most dangerous of all were those traitors who used me as their scapegoat, those without the courage to admit the power of my Act openly and so pretended to make a choice against it and to condemn it while, secretly, they joined me and craved me and wanted to imitate me. For these saw that I was acting out their own secret desires, and delivered to me the punishment which they felt would come to them if they made real, as I had, their own hidden reality. These were the killers who cried out that they were on the side of life and I on death's side, and they tried to murder me who symbolized what they did not have the courage to choose and face within themselves.

The great controversy began. One side said, "It is up to Marvello to disturb us, to speak for us"; the other said, "He is evil and mis-begotten and he shames us with his own obsessions." I came down, at nights, from the top of my tent, my work, into chaos and strife below. More and more I saw that my work in air, where I was re-moved and following the will of my own vision, solitary and in my innocent trance, was the only order I knew, and that I must make that choice: to stay with the work I was committed to and created for, to continue to bring the chaos and the strife and the betrayal on the ground to what order and what beauty and what simplicity I could in the air. Could my observers not see that every night I per-formed my Act I was brought to the very verge of destruction and that I saved myself, miraculously, whole and *rescued,* at that last per-ilous moment? They who had taught me what I had done could not see what they had taught me! But I was now, fully informed of my-self, ready to die for this work, let them hang me or burn me as infi-del or traitor or witch, it did not matter; I must do my work, over and withdrawn from it all, to inform it of error, to redeem it to meaning, and this through love. Now I was squarely confronting myself and my moral problem, for that was what it was. I went on, in my act, solitary and as myself, in my own style, and did not listen to the others.

But it was Pietro, my brother in the Act, who was determined to destroy me. Reduced, as it were, to ground and confined there by me who excelled him above in air, he envied and hated me. As I did my work above him I would occasionally catch the look of hatred in his face below, and tremble. One night, at the climax of my Act when every muscle and every nerve and sense in me was beating at the very edge of bursting in that final second of ecstasy which I knew in the Act, there rose up to me from below a far-off bellowing cry that resounded in the great tent: "CAIN!"; and in that second of ecstasy which is like a dying, the name was an ancient name deliver-ing me far back to my beginning. "CAIN!" it sounded once more, and all the evil of humanity was upon me like on blow. I lost my sense of myself and fell into the crowd.

Cries of "Marvello has fallen! Marvello has fallen!" echoed in my head as I fell, it seemed, through all the ages. How many were wounded by my fall and how many fatally I never knew, the figures changed so often as the reports came of the disaster; but many men and women were crippled by my fall. Where before a dazzling silver and blue bird had been my insignia, worn by my believers and admirers and converts on their hats or clothing, a crutch replaced it, upon which all the wounded walked. After my fall and the wounding of so many, a slow, wretched and haunted army of cripples left the city where I fell, and disappeared into the countries beyond.

I was maimed in the right leg and a look came into my face which has never left it, together with the look which was put into me by . . . whom? by my race? by the Flagpole Sitter in that other country, who, it seemed now, I had betrayed and destroyed? by Pietro? That mark lives there, in my face, as you can see, together with the other sign, half and half. But I had been named, and as I lay, healing, during those long long months of regeneration of the bone in a place, a sanctuary which I will later tell about, for that is in another country, I faced the name in myself and I came to know and to understand its meaning.

The night of the fall, among all the wailing, writhing victims in the darkness of the tent, in that terrible lightless night of destruction and tumult as if it were the clashing and the pandemonium of damned souls after the deluge or the fire, for a fire, too, was started by my fall, bodies were burned, survivors in rags were tearing at their hair and clutching onto the debris of demolished scaffolds, pulling themselves up, lovers were parted and called for one another and, finally, the whole flaming tent collapsed upon the agony of that tormented and suffering humanity, I crawled, like an animal, dragging my shattered limb behind me, out into the fields, through the fields and into the deep ditch alongside the Highway. I lay there all night, hearing the cries and screams and moans of the wounded and the terrified, hearing over and over again the cursing cry of "CAIN! CAIN!" in my ears, saw the blazing tent, my splendid ruined world, billow and fall into burning rags, heard the explosions around it, the piercing squalls of the beasts of the menagerie—alas, I had destroyed the whole living world, it seemed, and even the helpless animals—and I watched, like flaming Lucifer who fell to Earth, a torch to destroy it, the wounded and the killed pass by me on the Highway on litters and in ambulances or on the shoulders of rescuers. In my hallucinated agony I saw them carrying my magnificent master, Ishbel, away and it was then that I saw that he was the image of the Flagpole Sitter. I had not rescued and redeemed him at all—I had destroyed him. I wanted to die in my extreme agony and I tasted on my swollen tongue the green bile of death. I died in the ditch, as only the living can. My night passed . . . but into one long unrelieved darkness.

The next day, around noon, I dragged myself onto the Highway and, taken as one of the wounded, limping along the road in the company of my victims, because my face was so changed, the destroyer among the destroyed, unnoticed, I vanished. Where I went, I cannot tell; but I knew I had to heal myself, and that was my burden. I vanished; no one knew where I was, nor could anyone recognize my once famous and beautiful face, for there was the evil change over it, the look of Cain. I went up and down the world. I went to great cities. I dragged my crooked leg down the streets. I hid away. No one will ever know my agony in rooms.

Near one of the rooms I lived in—on a street of the afflicted: cripples, the blind, those suffering the misery and degradation of bodily beauty—was a hall where the crippled met for recreation. I peered through the window on the street, a ragged and haunted outcast, and felt my guilt again when I watched the cripples shambling through a Square Dance in their grotesque and mocking movements, and I felt I had crippled them. At the top of the window, when I looked up with tears on my fiendish face, I saw a painted sign which said, *"The way back is back to work."* And at that moment one of the twisted dancers in the hall saw my face at the window and fell to the floor as though his legs had been cursed by me and I had reminded him of his infirmity which he was slowly and patiently strengthening, in great faith; and the dance stopped. But the music, now a lingering ghostly tune of fiddlers, went on, and all the dancers turned and glared at my face in the window as if I were Satan. At that moment the music seemed the unearthly caterwaul of the lost souls of the damned, and it seemed that I had appeared to destroy this hopeful company struggling to recuperate themselves. I had no way back; I had no work except that which would only destroy again; and now even the look of my face would destroy. I turned and hobbled away, down the long cold cavern of the city street, among the blind, sweeping their way with sticks, tapping on the concrete, between the haunted buildings and through the knifeblades of winter wind that slashed at my flesh, leaving the dancers fallen and kicking on the floor in the Recreation Hall.

I had nobody to go to. If only I had had a friend to go to. But how could I dare to take a friend, I was so full of the fear that I would only wound him who would come close to me. They had convinced me, who so professed to love and desire and need me, that I was a dangerous man, a criminal, a killer, a destroyer. If love could do such damage, I thought, then what could hate do? If I could find someone to hate! I suddenly thought, that might change everything.

In the cities where I went, to my horror I saw little children in the streets and playgrounds imitating my Act. Its foul influence lingered in the world, even in the memory and mimicry of children as though I were some ancient mythic evil or an infamous desperado become a hero of bad children. I have corrupted the whole living world, I thought, and huddled and shambled away. In another city, on Twelfth Night, masquers were chasing a scarlet Devil, and when the Bride and Groom ran suddenly upon me in the street they withdrew in dread and then, joined by their wedding guests, fell upon me and beat me when I could not run. If I went into churches, the very Crucifix seemed to be the shape of the Ishbel Family Act and mocked me, skull and bones at the foot of it. I crept, bent, in horror out of the churches. And I asked myself again, who had killed Marvello? What had brought him down? What had caused his fall?

I made money in ways too horrible to speak of. At night I committed animal acts upon whatever victim would take me, in the pitch dark; and on Sundays I sat by the door of a church and begged with my half-look of love. My face had gone that once had been so beautiful on posters for all to see. I had the feeling it had, being one of two faces like those on cards, been turned over to the other side by some gambler hand. Why was I different? What did these others, who passed me on the sidewalks and peered at me from windows, know or have that I did not? Where was I so wrong, so outcast by being simply what I was, and they seemingly so right? I thought, if I am that name that destroyed me—*who* called it up to me?—then I will murder, after the work of the bearer of that name. I murdered, in the way purity can be corrupted, to remind men of Cain.

Once, as I scraped against a body pressed to a dark wall in an alleyway of a great city, rubbing as if I were to rub off all the evil and guilt of me onto it, I looked, with my swimming eye of animal ecstasy just at the moment when I might lose, for one flash of sensual oblivion, all my soul's sorrow, upon the dark and scabby wall where I had my lover pinned, into the face of one I had long ago known (somewhere, where?), like an ancestor. The eyes were ogled upwards in sensual joy just as mine were at that moment of looking, and the face was scarred as if clawed by the nails of a wild beast; and over the wild, umbrageous and defiled face were written the half-effaced letters of a name: Marvello. It was my face on an advertisement of my lost and destroyed Act. In that second of my wailing joy-grief I found myself again and it was as if I were again in the climax of my Act at the top of the tent. I cried "Marvello!" and then I crumpled down at the feet of my despised and blessed lover. My lover, stunned and terrified, fled down the dark alleyway and abandoned me there, alone with my dishonored image on the wall.

But I continued my criminal life. What I began with strangers in tenderness, at which they marveled as they loved me, in sighs and fierce embraces and whispered praises and protestations, ended in what I saw, afterwards, had been my hatred, and ended in violence: I crippled them. For invariably strangers would want to know who I was, who could love so passionately and give so much of myself to strangers. Some of them said, "You will die by love"; others said I had invited them to murder me in love. "Who are you?" they would ask, with a flushed and trembling face of overwhelming passion. Then when I could not tell them, for who *was* I?, they turned on me. Or even if I told them who I was, I was telling a lie, for I myself did not know who I was; and if a union began with someone based upon what I declared myself to be, for I was so vaunted because of my superb animalism—and this led me to begin to make impetuous declarations—then in time the union crumbled under violence because I was not what I said, or thought I was. "Save me! save me!" I began to cry out to my lovers who tore at my flesh; and what I meant was "name me!" I, again, was their sensuality's scapegoat which they at once fought and drew to them but would not admit in the daylight. They wanted to keep me as the evil part of themselves, denying my existence within them but using me, as if they were using themselves in a dark closet. This was their murder, for they were my killers: this is how I found my murderers. Who crippled who, then? "Bring me alive! Come alive with me! Let us name each other, honestly and without guilt!" I would cry. "Let us be wild together, anything, but surrender with me. I cannot live death—and when I die, like this, as you see me, dying, it is not even death, that is the evil of it, it is not even death." But they would not know what I meant, they would not understand and only said, "Love me again, quickly!" I loved through half a race, hunting my murderer. I knew I had to be brought to life, to my reality again through love, if I could find the one who would die with me and bring a resurrection, a rising to life: one who would admit and face the Cain in me and in all others and with me seek our common brotherhood. I loved through all that race of dead and killing lovers, murderers. I had known the beautiful things we human beings can do to one another.

But I had not found my Marvello, and so what Self I had to give to others was a lost Self, an avenging Self, and who would join me, lost himself, to find that, together? Cain—that name—is the lost part of us all. I tell you we must heal the Cain in us, and we must do it together. This is what I had to learn. Someone to be true with! I cried out to myself. Someone with whom to make a choice and together keep it! Someone through whom to see all that had happened to me and to whom to relate all that happened and with whom to be in a human connection of all honesty, who would understand my crimes which I was committing *towards them!* It was as though I was loving myself towards this other. Together we would make a new beginning, a new world.

So I had, again, and by my nature, begun to attract to me another race of half-livers and half-lovers, and this time, again, I was one of them, stronger now, more lost than ever, turned upon myself, striking out at myself to try to destroy myself. I was in a relationship with those half-people who swarm and cluster round a desirable object off which they can suckle and who are more murderous than the criminal. I invited them and turned themselves upon themselves and they turned myself upon me, in the very fields of love. But slowly, now, I was beginning to see that my only recourse was to utter exile, where I might live in and move in that innocence, lost to me, and in that undisturbed connection with the living air-world through which alone anything that lives can thrive and find its own growth, where my two half-faces might have a conversation and unite to make a whole face. Where were the undisguised? Where was anyone who had the strength and the courage to show himself as he was? The only hope, the only salvation, I knew now, was to find everything in my own self, where I had found so much evil and damage, to make that choice and to keep it, and to find it at my beginnings. But that was a crooked way home, where I was going.

If I could recapture the heroic feelings I had when so long ago I saw the figure on the flagpole and had my heroic dream of him, I might be the man I had thought to be! But I lost it, that *feeling* of the idea, and the idea alone was cold and fleshless; I could not *be* an idea where the blood had run out of it and love had died in it. How to put love back into it? Considering how I look at human experience, my own experience, when I discover myself's way of seeing what happens, am I doomed to ruin a magnificent vision because I live up too high over it, climbing up there to look at it because from where I look there is that slanting angle of my view which I seemed cursed by and which conflicts with what is seen from other points and levels? What will be the fortune of my image, its progress through use in the world and through my constant examination of it, if it employs me to *its* ends, if I lose control of the image, if it hallucinates me?

If one could again have a marvelous dream, or *create* one, and within that find something of value to go by, keeping it alive, and making it real and substantial in the walking world! If one could discover a society to move with! But we do not seem to be going in the same direction. The only thing is to take the dangerous chance and choice: to create or help recreate a society from my own sources and living close to them, alienated from those sources of the world which seem to be fed by a falling poison, like slow dew, strangling men. So many others have made up a world and through that regenerated an afflicted world, and have done it alone in their own artifice. Out of their fantastic notion came a third world, re-moved from the fantastic creator and the world he sat or walked in as he created it, yet born out of the half-murderous relationship of two lovers. For both had to begin with love; and an expression of *both*, an *object*, a living third, speaking for both but removed, clear and permanent, resulted—to which they and others could refer what happened in their conflict with each other, and which would clarify it: an idea of flesh and blood to go by, to rescue with, and to influence to understanding.

This is my choice . . .

—London

at lady a.'s
(THE PATIENT'S NOTEBOOK)

1

We were in Lady A.'s apartment drinking wine, and she was speaking of "muddlers," in her incessant and indefatigable style of long unpunctuated utterances, stumbling sometimes through heavy underbrush of her laughter but triumphantly blazing her trail out again with chopping hatchets of phrases into the clear sunlight and treeshade of her discourses. She was a nervous and beautiful little trailblazer and wilderness-breaker of a woman whose conversation—or monologue—was a physical exercise which gave her a good workout, taking such control of her at times that it would throw her into fits of coughing and collision with objects in the room, vases, chairs, ashtrays; but she fought it through, as though she might be chasing her conversation about the room; and in the end it lay exhausted on the floor, among the breakage and the casualties of the pursuit, while she, puffing and straightening her hair and her clothing, lighted another cigarette with the final "you see"; and here her witness, her listener, was able to rush in, like a stretcher-bearer, to carry the whole thing away, a "yes!"

"You will not let a thing alone until you have nudged it and tickled it and excited it into such a sensational, moiled-up mess that you no longer know, yourself, what it meant at first, and *it* takes hold of *you*; you will not let a thing follow its own life, you twist it and wrench it and hurry it and blow it up until you *make* it true and you have us all believing it is true, until, one by one, we find you out. Deliver yourself of this infernal idea, honey, come down to your human race that inhabits the earth, that walks on the green ground; you are so sweet; that look in your face; that adorable face; have some more wine, honey. When I was in Paris in the Twenties I drank only this good wine; and yesterday, just suddenly, I found it again in a little shop on Lexington Avenue and bought a whole case, made the man go straight down in the cellar, honey, and bring up the whole god-damned thing; I know a good thing when I see it, and what I love finally comes round back to me, isn't it strange how what we love and lose for a long time comes back again? Suddenly there it is, honey, and all we have to do is reach out and take it back for ourselves. Oh honey I spilled a little, that precious good wine, but that's all right, just lean down and lick it up, honey, hahahahaha, that's right; oh honey don't we have a good time? Honey it's a man's world and look what they have done to it, debased and insulted the women until they no longer have any dignity, womankind; but honey they won't whip me, the nasty little clayeaters—once they taste the stuff, like those clayeaters in Georgia, they won't take anything else. Oh hon-nee!—don't look that way, why do we live so badly when we've got all God's green world; hon-nee drink your wine. That good wine has all Paris in it, has all the Twenties in it, has all the people I loved and was gay with in it, it's like seeing old friends again to drink

drink this precious wine; it's a bad world, honey, we've got now, a vile heap of bones, I want to die, how I despise the world we've made for ourselves, honey, where is our human life? Don't you be another basket case, do you hear me, you stay good and true, you're strong honey though when I first knew you I thought the world would kill you if you just walked down its streets; but you're tough, darling. If you'd just *listen* to me, I don't know why you don't listen to me—now I'm talking like your mother, honey, but I don't feel about you like a mother, you understand?—and get this idea out of your head and grow into the man you were meant to be, what did your mother and father do to you when you were young that you haven't grown into the man you were meant to be? What did somebody do to you? Honneeee! There's not a thing I can do for you, you won't listen to me, you won't let me tell you something, I can't do a thing in this world for you, hon-neee! You won't let a thing alone until you have killed it . . . Oh hon-neee! hon-neee!"

2

I have just come from a party at Lady A.'s. I must say that the quarrel between Lady A. and her friend, the literary one with the pearl on a silver chain around his neck, threatened to usurp the evening from the other guests—the quarrel was, again, about men's betrayal of women—until he, the "Brother" of what he and Lady A. call their "Brother and Sister Act" (they frequently amuse Literary and Ladies' Groups in the city with lectures and aesthetic opinions) finished the whole thing by saying, passionately, "If our women are suffering because of this breakdown in their men, their relations with them seem to be acts of terrorization in the ruins, of carpetbagging and vandalism." And someone, the woman who ran an art gallery, I believe, laughed so loud and rushed into an opinion of her own that I was unable to hear the rest.

The art gallery woman, who had a weeping voice and a competitive temperament towards her artists, was saying how she thought young painters ought to share the experience "of their time"; and I answered that the experience of an artist's "time" was his *own* experience and that no one could "want" an artist to "have experience"; that he finds his own. But the gallery woman went on to say that the homosexuality of so many young artists doomed them. Lady A., far away at the other end of the long room, caught that word and responded, rushing over to the conversation.

"They have never really done anything lasting," she chimed. "Somerset Maugham has said that what they do has only the glitter of tinsel . . . As for the artist's experience, look at the Twenties."

I answered that there are many ways of love and that it might seem true that any way of love, however outside the pattern of the majority, might be less destructive than the perversities of lovelessness. Lady A. rankled across at me and said, through her laughter, "Honey why don't you go on over to their side, you're always defending them . . ."

At this point there was the ring of the doorbell, and when the door was opened, in flapped a beaky woman as though she had been let into a cage of birdseed, who cried out, arms in the air, "New York, New York!" She was a kind of newspaper writer about art, a journalist who wrote pieces about the new painting ("the trembling reds, the pulsing yellows, the vibrant ultra-marines and siennas, the subtle mauves, the electric etc. etc. etc."), who had got herself into the theatrical circle as well and felt she had worthy opinions about plays and performances.

"I am late and I need a drink," she explained, pecking hellos to the party people and hopping about the room in a cabbagey taffeta skirt. "A friend of mine is trying to leave her husband and I have been going through *all that*" (she had her cultivated mannerism of growling words she wished to emphasize) "all evening—it made me miss my dinner, but I hope you all had something exQUIsite" (she growled again). "As for me, I had olives and gherkins—out of my martinis—and I need more."

She was doused momentarily with a drink, but, the first gulp down, she flung herself directly into the competition of opinions that was flourishing in the room, had something to say about every subject that was brought up, had seen this preview, had read the script of that new play, knew, even, the author, he was a "fabulous person," "quite mad," a poet, and Broadway was too literal for him, Broadway was not "ready for him, yet," but she had "met him at drinks" yesterday, bringing to one the image of a water trough, and said, among other things to him, "don't you know an artist has to be tough, he has to be a fighter"; but, nevertheless, he had gone on one of his drinking cycles despite the injections the famous new woman doctor in the city had been giving him. It had ended with his vomiting on the floor at *Cheerios*. She and a good friend from TIME who was in his same corner at *Cheerios*, singing the same song *"Mama don't 'low no boy-girls in here"* and then bursting out in rages of attacks on the job he had been forced to take with that magazine and which was killing him, but he would die in *Cheerios* or, if that was too crowded, in *Costellos*, "exercising his elbow."

The hoary old publisher, over from England, was commenting to a few listeners on that young American writer, tragic and delicate and very ill, who was "taking England"—as though she might be sacking that country, as Alaric had Rome; and he ended by saying "who will stop her?", so that one was sure that she was invading England. "Will she ever write again?" he asked; and added a few comments on the history of the passport, how someone should write a book about that. His wife, a gawky and towering woman dressed entirely in red, with a wide flannel mouth, red again, stood by absolutely silent and grieved-looking and she appeared to be an effigy of herself already in flames.

An anthologizer was there, and he brought up poetry; and they were all going to have to talk about that. It began, and I withdrew as I heard the woman art writer telling everybody that she knew the British poet X personally and had met him at drinks last week and told him that he ought to write a long ballad about New York, he was the one to do it.

I withdrew to a corner chair below a modern painting of a nude young man—except for ballet slippers—of large sex and a boyish face. I was glad the blonde woman named Lucy came to join me soon, and we began to speak about living in New York.

"It is a dangerous place, I know," she said, twisting her cigarette round with thumb and forefinger as though she were dialing a safe. "But there are its little coves and caves one can take refuge in."

"What do you do here?" I asked.

She told me she was a writer. She said she wanted to leave the party shortly to go Downtown to hear some jazz, and would I like to go with her? I said I would like it.

We left shortly, and quietly, only nodding to Lady A., not wanting to disrupt the discussion now, which sounded to be about Hemingway. The woman art writer was telling how she had met him in Havana and discussed Miró with him.

Lucy and I came to the apartment building in the Village. When the door opened, there was an assortment of young people huddled together in the large room where the saxophone player, whose name was Jack, lived. Jack kissed Lucy hello and greeted me. We came into another conversation.

A youngish, rather tortured-looking red fellow was telling the others about his views on sex. "A faggot should be screwed at least once by a woman . . ." he said, just like that.

"Just try it Baby and see where you get . . ." a tall, yellow wild-looking girl replied; and the group laughed a little. They were drinking beer and Lucy and I were given a glass of it. The conversation went on . . . where was the jazz? . . . and it was about writers and sex, the sexual habits and predilections of those present. Writers were named—"Him? Oh sure! He's gay as pink ink." "D . . . ? Well, that's another thing. D's afraid, but he's queer, you can be sure of that. I know people who know . . ."

"In New York, sex is no problem; you can have what you want and you can find it anywhere," a young man with a scarf wound round his neck declared.

"He is Paul Plovers," Lucy told me, "and his first novel was a best-seller." She named it but I had only heard its title.

"But as for me, I've had enough to last me a while," the young novelist divulged. "I've got to get out of this fucking Village, it's killing me."

"Where will you go, Pauly baby?" the wild girl, who was now sitting astride his outstretched leg with her arm around his neck, asked his mouth, and then kissed it.

"Rome," he said. "I can't work here."

"That's where they all are," the girl said. "They've moved their camp there for the winter." She pouted a second, then mewed, "But Baby what will I do?"

"Listen to this woman," the novelist told the others. "I know what you'll do, honey; what you can't live without doing and what you can do best. Fuck. You love it too much to do without it. That's why I love you," he added, patting her thigh . . . .

The bunch laughed; and then the discussion was about contraceptives. They argued them, some in favor, others cursing them. I was not so much embarrassed as I was self-conscious, and particularly because of Lucy. But Lucy whispered to me that there was nothing wrong with such a conversation, to "quit being so sensitive."

Suddenly there was the sound of two conversations, one cutting across the other, and it was because Jack had pulled out his recording machine from under the bed where he had recorded the whole conversation. The group hushed. The conversation played on, and its hollow resounding gave the feeling that the speakers were all in a deep cistern, talking and talking and talking. Finally the red young man shouted, "Turn off that goddamned thing, I didn't say that!" He leaped from his chair and ran for the recording machine. But Jack intercepted him and they grappled and struggled, while the others sat perfectly calm and still and the conversation played on and on . . . Lucy and I crept out.

As we walked down the street, I said to Lucy, "You're tough."

"Sure. I had to get that way. This city nearly killed me at first, and I had to get tough. You will, too."

We went by taxi to her apartment and I took her up four flights to her door; and though I was longing to go in with her and stay the rest of the night with her, I held back, and so did Lucy; and we said goodnight, dishonestly, at the door.

—New York

It was the second day of Chris's coma, and the rains had begun again, this time torrential. I began to work around the heart of Chris.

As our hospital was situated in a low place, by noon the waters had begun to rise. It was as though Chris and I were safe in a dry cove under a waterfall. I began to manipulate the loom, this time in the area of his breast, for his heart was struggling. We were in that territory, where our conversation went on. Now it seemed that the working of the loom was the turning of a wheel that caused the flooding of a memory and could bring, through struggle, rescue from it.

Was it error that I took my subject so to myself? Did hallucination or vision, out of lonely judgment, follow: I can only put down what happened.

By nightfall, the waters of the flood had risen already to the level of the second floor, where we were, and we knew the night would be a perilous one, because the rains still poured down upon us. We began to make plans for evacuation to the third and topmost floor if that should become necessary. Chris hung above the level of the water, dry and safe, coming slowly to life on the loom I worked. All the earth seemed covered with water and my weaving movements were like the rowing of a boat with my patient as my passenger.

We should have known a flood was coming, because for a whole week before the rains all the animals knew it was coming. You never heard so many bullfrogs in all Kingdom; crickets and treefrogs, too, were calling and sobbing all night long; and scrootch-owls scrootching. And all during the first night of Chris's coma one lone frog sobbed and sobbed outside below his window, like a human voice, as I worked the loom round Chris's head. The zoo, a mile away, was unhappy and troubled, the nervous horses stamped and snorted their heads, the cats called and the elephants sounded their baleful trumpets. It was a disturbed night. The men's wounds augured bad weather, too, and so I was reminded again of the connection between animal and human wounding. It had been so dry. The very land cracked and was like an old face—if you have ever noticed an old face, how it is like the ground. But never you mind, the drought was broken, and then some, and for a long time.

The first rain was green rain, if you've ever seen it; but the whole world, trees and houses and grass, seemed yellow. It was going to be a catastrophe, and we should have known it. The limbs of the patients knew it, where the patients did not. But the animals had known it first. They always do, yet it is said they have no minds.

By nightfall we began the evacuation to the top floor. The children were first, and the little Preacher, Lord Bottle, was preaching passionately in his sleep as we carried him up, crying out between exhortations, "Nurse, Nurse, bottle! bottle!"; and of course this sermon, a special one for us all, rising out of the extraordinary circumstances, touched on the Flood. The ambulatory patients went in a slow line on their crutches, complaining of their wounds, and because of the fragility of the patients, the removal took hours, as they moved like sleepwalkers, and many of them were half-asleep or under their nighttime sedation. It was all very quiet and trancelike, without the slightest confusion or panic, as though we were acting out some prophecy; there was the rhythm and spell of dreamlike dancing about it all, as though each man carried a tune in his head to keep time to. The only sound was that of the thundering rain like the rolling of many deep waves. We decided to move Chris among the last, and so while he was waiting for his turn, I worked very hard round his heart to make it strong enough to move him, navigating his wooden bed with the tent over it as if it were a boat and I rowing him through the waters, a long ways.

As I looked out the window onto the turbulent waters of the rising flood where we had searchlights to watch the rising level, I never before or after saw such a sight. Animals began floating by, because the zoo was wrecked and all the animals aloose. Nurses and Internes and what patients could help stood on the second-story gallery and quietly, as if in a dream, snatched to salvation every living animal they could lay hands on. They threw lifelines into the teeming waters and never knew what might be brought in: the big front room at the far end of the second floor was like a menagerie—this was where they led the animals that came in as though they were welcome and in the utmost pacification. In came the lions and the giraffes, the elephants and the hippopotamuses, the whole benevolent kingdom; and now the hospital seemed to move, like the heart of Chris, to be riding along on the crest of the flood with all this strange cargo and population, this sanctuary. We knew there must be gigantic destruction all outside, since the remnants and wreckage of it rode and bobbled past us through the light of the searchlights. Still they came in as they were rescued out of the waters, all the peaceful animals, birds and even marvelous snakes who did not even show their wicked tongues, they were so grateful it seemed; and little blinking monkeys were brought in, sheep, every kind of animal you can imagine. And as they were led through the ward, they were mingled with the quiet and benign procession of the delicate wounded men, they all went out together.

Pretty soon we began to see people floating by and they were pulled in, too, when they could be caught. The waters kept rising and rising and the torrent falling, the way a fall causes a rise. One man that was saved and brought into our sanctuary—coming by holding on to a floating door that seemed, in the searchlight, to be a door of light—when he was snatched in and dried off, said he saw rafts floating and got on one, saw two eyes, said "who's on this raft with me," and 'twas a bear. He got off in a hurry. Said he saw another raft and got on it and there was a great big snake. He said he got off quick. "Well," his rescuers said, "they're both in there, in the other room, the bear and the snake; we saved them." And he did not say a word, the rescued man. Another, a woman, told us that the Italians were all in the trees in the dark, calling *Io morrò! Io morrò!*

How the building stood I'll never know. Occasionally it shuddered with the stiff twisting of the waters, but otherwise it rode them as lightly as a buoy. Yet it was filled with all this humanity and life. More people were pulled in. Children who had lost their parents but hoped to find them upstairs in this sanctuary, delicate old men holding to their breast a little hen or cock like a drop of feathers, or a drenched staring old cat under their arms; two wilted little nuns looking as though all the starch had been rinsed out of them, wearing their habits like drenched wings; and so many more.

With all the quiet suffering and the dumbshow traffic of the crippled, the drowning, and the washing away, all I could really think of was what was poor Chris dreaming through it all, in his other country, alone through it all. He is the only safe one, really, I thought, for he is up above and over and clear of all this washing water down below him. I kept a watch on him to see if he might make some sign to say that he was coming down from his coma that raised him above it all; but there was not yet any sign, he was closed up in his dry tent. I worked round his heart until the time to move him away in his bed to the third floor. Once, I turned to see a huge and hideous hippo coming through the window, he had been helped up out of the flood, and someone said he was the ugliest creature God created. But one of the refugees, a little old bent gray man who had just been brought up saved, said, "These creatures are the most sensitive and delicate of all. Do not let them hear you speak of their repugnance, for they live among men only through love, and if they sense that they are ridiculed, they will die." The gentle hippo went on his way, led by someone, to the menagerie in the far room. But soon, because it was feared that the second story would be engulfed, the animals were moved up the stairs. We heard the ghostly sounds of the great hooves and clawed feet on the steps. When I navigated Chris in his bed into the large wide third-floor sanctuary, I saw a lovely sight: the patients were in one end, quiet and at rest, and at the other end of the room the large beautiful family of animals, every kind, was gathered together, some lying, some sitting, some standing licking themselves dry or resting or licking others dry—there was the clean odor of wet fur—the whole company of the sanctuary had made friends and there was a harmony and a goodwill among all that household, the peaceable kingdom.

We rode through the flood for days and days, no one knew how long. I certainly don't remember. Everybody helped with the preparation of food and with the housekeeping, and the household of animal and wounded flourished.

We rode the flood, and I waited for some sign from Chris. But he rode it like a buoy, rocking as I rolled him gently from side to side upon the loom I worked. As I tended his notebook, too, I left Chris to look into it for another sign to go by.

I found some pages written in Venice, for "Venice," and a date, were signed at the end of the writing. What I read rose up into my head like a cry of Proteus out of the waters and sank back again. Something was rescued by Chris, in Venice, I saw, and again, there in the ward:

the wounding of my ancestry
(THE PATIENT'S NOTEBOOK)

I think of my grandmother's house in the city where she had moved from Trinity County, and she has given me the money in a little black purse and the list to buy at the store, the same things: a loaf of Wonderbread with the colored glasses inside the wrapper and postcard pictures of fishes and birds to be looked at through them; and a fifteen-cent soup bone. I can hear her deaf woman's flat voice crying "Why don't any of my children ever come to see me?" as she sat in her rocking chair with one leg folded under her, the guitar like a baby across her lap. In the next room, but not the one where Beatrice lay moaning with her headache that never seemed to let her alone and for which they had scarred her beautiful face with operations to try to find the source of her misery, I can hear my grandmother sing "I'll Be No Stranger There" as she played the guitar; and looking at the wreck of the sleeping porch with so many beds and cots—for Beatrice's two children, for Fay's two, for me, for my grandmother, for my grandfather who would not stay home, for Fay and for Jock—I think of the plight of the kitchen with the boiler of kidney beans on the stove and the roaches running, the dripping faucet that stained the sink rustcolored, and of the backyard where the fig trees smell rotten and the damp weeds steam in the hot sun, and the pervading odor of Natural Gas sours the air.

Then I hear Beatrice's voice calling me, flat like her mother's, as though she too were deaf. But she was so very beautiful, blonde silken hair that fell in locks around her enormous blue eyes . . . and her scarred face over which she wore a veil, as if she were masked, even in bed—I see her blue eyes peeping over the edge of the veil as if it were a wall, and the broken hole of mouth when she drew deep breaths of pain, the trembling of the veil when she cried out. "Chris, please Chris, come to your Aunt Beatrice, she is so sick."

I go into her sad room where her husband had not set foot for many months, he had disappeared, though Aunt Fay's, her third, was around the house all the time, having no job nor seeming to want any, and he was a young Seaman with tattoos and still wearing his Seaman's pants, Jock was his name, he cursed and was restless, would come and go or lie on the bed he and Fay slept in on the sleeping-porch with all the rest—only the children could hear what they thought was Jock beating Fay in the night, crying out to her and panting "you f—!"— smoking and reading from a storage of battered Western and Romance Stories magazines under the bed. "Please help your Aunt Beatrice get a little ease from this headache; reach under the mattress here—don't tell anybody, Chris, your Aunt Beatrice has to have some rest from this pain—reach right here under the mattress and give me that little bottle. That's it. This is our secret, Chris, and you must never tell anybody."

Why should this beautiful Beatrice have to die in a Rest Home, alone and none of her family ever coming to see her until they sent a message that she was dead? But I thought, then, that if I had, secretly, helped ease her suffering, I had that to know, without telling—until I heard them say that she had died from taking too much medicine from a hidden bottle, and where did she get it and who gave it to her?

Now we are riding, at midnight or later, my grandmother and I in the old car I went to college in, as fast as I can drive it, my little old gasping grandmother no bigger than a hen huddled in the seat beside me, clucking and clutching at my knee, moaning "Hurry, hurry, Chris, your grandmother is dying; God will bless you for this! That none of my children would come to me when I called" (she had called so many times), "and that my grandson came to take me to where I can die in peace, the Lord will bless him. Hurry, hurry, Chris, your grandmother is choking to death. You go on to college, Chris, and don't let them make you go to work, you get your college education and you won't be like the rest of them. . . ." The rain was still falling as it had been for a week, it was Spring, and the charity hospital was on the banks of the bayou which had overflown and flooded the road: the hospital seemed to be rising on the water and floating like a huge lighted ship. When the waters came to the running board of the car, we stalled and could go no farther, and I took the light little shrugged-up shape in my arms and carried her through knee-deep water, reaching the hospital.

We went in the emergency entrance and found water on the floor; but the charity patients, some Mexicans, some Negroes, some poor countryfolk, were sitting or lying on the benches waiting for the Nurses. My grandmother kept choking and gasping, "Tell them to hurry, Chris." They finally carried her to a ward, I helping. While they got her to bed, I sat in the waiting room hearing the rain and going from time to time to the window to look out on the rising flood of the bayou. I saw animals in distress, floating and swimming, and one of the Nurses told me that the polluted waters of the bayou had caused a sickness, a kind of plague, for the water supply of the surrounding section of the city had been contaminated, and did my grandmother have the sickness? "No," I answered, "she is just very old and worn out from trying to die so many times." And when I turned and said, "Please let her die," the Nurse answered that she had died, calling to Beatrice.

I put this down because I have suddenly remembered it here in this city built on water, and because tonight as I was going up the magnificent stairway to the Princess Galvana's dinner party I suddenly smelled the odor of kidney beans cooking and I heard my grandmother's voice crying "Hurry, Chris, hurry, your grandmother is dying," and I felt compelled to turn back and go away. But for what reason? I reasoned with myself, and so went on. At dinner I overturned my wine glass three times, embarrassing even the butler, running with napkins, the third time. Several Americans were there: Lady A., though, was the only one I knew; a beautiful harelipped woman artist, and a fortyish, effeminate litterateur who kept speaking of the prizes some committee, of which he was Chairman, was going to bestow shortly on promising young writers. Lady A. kept being called to the telephone in the next room, returning the last time to say, "Paris—I'm afraid we're going to run into war over oil in Persia."

—Venice

We rode the flood, this strange company, and we seemed to flourish. But a woman we had rescued fell in love, it was reported, with a bird, a splendid imperial Swan; and one young rescued man, who grew restless and impatient, escaped from the sanctuary (we did not try to stop him, every man did as he pleased) by means of wings he made for himself out of feathers of some of the birds and out of plaster of paris used for the casts of broken limbs. We saw him sail for a moment and then fall into the flood. And there was a sullen man who had some hidden feeling in him which we could not understand, and in the days that followed we watched him rankle and knew that he felt malice towards someone of the company. One night he tried to murder another man who, so far as we could make out, had not committed one unseemly act.

In time, groups were formed, certain of the refugees emerged as leaders with causes and others became their followers, there was dissension between the groups; and so we saw that we had the same race of men as had existed before the flood. For a while we thought we might be beginning a new world. There seemed no other that had not been destroyed by the catastrophe of water, and we seemed the only humanity surviving. But soon we saw that in the sanctuary there was going to be the same world over again.

There was a report that a stranger in a boat had done a heroic job of rescuing people from houses and trees and rooftops. It was now known that he had brought people and animals in his boat, and even some few precious objects which he thought worthy of saving back from the destruction of the water. Who was this rescuer? He was searched for among the company, but no one like him was to be found. Then had he drowned, this rescuer, had he lost his life in the rescue? The people he had saved tried to describe him, but each description, vague and undetailed, contradicted the other, and in the end we had no more than a sense of the rescuer. Some said they had seen him somewhere before, but they did not know where.

We knew we were safe, so long as the building survived, what with the animals who know more about the catastrophes of nature than we humans. In time, they would know what to do; they would leave when it was time and safe, so we depended on the animals.

During the flood, I worked round the heart of Chris; and as I did my work in this country of him, I imagined a sad and lovely tale to see if it might speak for him and for this region of his mysterious world that lay in my claim as though I had seized or conquered it and now ruled it like an Emperor. Given as much as I had read from him, my imagination began to collaborate with him; and hearing as much as I had heard from him, from that voice beneath his body, the human cry of that face which I heard as I looked at him, I began to try to speak with it or to speak to it, or to answer it. I began to create, or to *re-create* a world for this body to live in. This face of flesh and bone was yet a face of earth, like the ground and what composes it: clay, quarry, dirt; and like what grows in the ground: weed, grass, leaf. But we all of us know that something, some power, can bring this flesh of clay and grass beyond its common substance into a race of legendary people, a people of larger-than-human stature and bearing, and then deliver it back to what withers and dies, or stays forever. A man who makes such a being raises him to a triumphant sense of self through this very gesture. It is this gesture which pervades and surrounds and emanates from what is created or made up. This is the hand, the inventing hand which, as if in great danger itself (and you see the danger), had seized out of pandemonium this ordered image, had snatched it out, whole and safe and undamaged from chaos to give it; the hand is safe, we know, but it quickly obliterates its gesture of salvation or any attention to its own heroic act and withdraws itself, leaving only the rescued image which has, now, taken on a *sense of its rescuer,* and adds that to its own meaning. It is this quality of the *marvel* of which I speak. I think you see the process of this construction out of a destruction, the way repair works: your object and subject (for they are one) seems at once about to disintegrate and yet to order itself out of its fragments with astonishing simplicity and through the means of one simple shape or form as the center around which the whole design clusters and from which it takes its larger shape. In the end, this simple, residual shape seems to have been seized at the verge of disintegration and rescued back into order. After one has been in the company of his subject for a while, his subject seems to have been saved from his unutterable peril and to have been rescued from his disturbed tensions and intensities and sufferings and passions aloft into a permanent and liberated air of grace, informed with his own sense of what he has been rescued from. For this subject is, finally, one who has suffered through, together with his creator and savior, what has happened to him, what he carries within himself, his terrible and beautiful vision which he has had no fear of showing; and he has arrived at this permanent instant of integration at which his creator sees him there in his now fearless and indestructible totality of *himself.* The subject has not been surrealized or intellectualized or psychoanalyzed. To look at your invented one or to live with him for a while is to have to submit to the processes at work within him, for he shows you an active, dynamic experience of a growing, searching, suffering process, and to come through with him, in the end. This was my objective with my patient.

Now we were both, Chris and I, in great danger and in that perilous and delicate balance of which I have spoken. In the service of the idea of Chris, I saw how my idea had taken on a moral reality all its own, speaking for itself, beyond me and independent of me, and it began to add to my invention. What I felt I had rescued, or was rescuing, had taken on the sense of its rescuer and added that to itself.

But would my idea ever walk on two feet and go its own way, or would it end the ghost of an idea, and forever an invalid, to whom my ghostly voice would call out, "*Be* my idea of you!" I continued my collaboration with him . . .

The House on the River,
or: The Construction East of Town

The house was in a city near the town where he was born. It had many gables and roofs like tents on a cliff, and it sat at the edge of a drop, at the foot of which ran a wide American river. Beyond it and below, in the lowlands, was the city. He had wandered there.

He lived, for a little while, in a rooming house in the city. There lived in this house a young girl named Stella, a student at the nearby University. They kept apart, though when they met on the stairway they flashed eyes. There was, even in their first such meeting, if it can be called that, this dialogue of eyes, that soft hairy speech of lash and lid. There was something between them. The story of their falling in love is very beautiful.

One day, as he left his room, which was at the head of the first landing of the stairs—his room broke off at this landing and turned away from it into an isolated wing of the house—he saw below, at the front door, Stella putting on her boots before going out. He knew they would meet at the door, and for a moment he was afraid and thought to turn back and go into his room to wait until she had left. But he went ahead down the stairs and towards the door. When he got there, Stella looked up at him and he kept her eyes; and for the first time they looked each other daringly full in the face. She was exquisitely beautiful, fragile moist face, large swollen lips and deep dark eyes. He could not move on. They stood there—how long?—and then he managed to unlock himself from the embrace of her eyes and go out. Suddenly, outside, he did not know where to go. Where *was* there to go, at that moment, except back to her? Any place where Stella was not, was of no purpose, he knew now. Now, in that moment, he knew clearly how he had sat in his room and longed to be with her, how he had listened for her feet on the stairs that passed his room, why he had not slept at night, knowing that her room was just up the next small flight of stairs and across, at a diagonal, from his. He knew, now, what he had not admitted to himself, that he had dreamed of her, night after night, and that he longed to have a conversation with her, to find her out, to bring her into his room and lock the door and live, day after day, a secret life with her. At this moment, standing on the porch just outside the closed door on the other side of which Stella bent, clasping her boots, while Chris rolled up the collar of his coat in the cold snowy air, he knew what all his dreams and all his restlessness had been about. Suddenly the door opened and Stella appeared on the porch. When she had closed the door, she looked full at him again; and Chris said to her, softly, "We already have so much between us . . . Stella." She said, shyly and tenderly, "I know."

They walked away together, through the quiet falling snow. She was going with him, he knew and she knew it. They were walking towards the Park and in the opposite direction from the University, her destination. Suddenly she spoke.

"The Landlady says you are a poet."

"I want to be," he answered, looking into the snow.

They walked on, silently. At the Park, they went under the trees and found a bench to sit on. He noticed now that she was wearing dungarees and a black sweatshirt, and that when she took off her black stocking cap she had a head of closely cropped tangled black hair. She was fragile and boylike. Chris embraced her gently, and then what he had held back, as in captivity, even without knowing, broke wild aloose, and he loved her so fiercely that he could hardly remember anything more of it than a blotting and blacking out of all that white, still landscape, that frozen pond before them upon which they had both seen, standing and watching them, but had not spoken of, a tall-legged spectral white bird as if it were a frozen figure of ice that had been a fountain out of whose beak water fell in the summer. It was the first time of love for her and Chris had not known it would be; nor did he really know it had been, it was all so savage and he was so deaf with his desires, until afterwards. But he knew, later, that she had been waiting towards him as he had towards her, except they had taken different paths of waiting. Afterwards, they waited, deaf and dumb; and then still without any words between them, they got up and walked back towards the house. They both knew where they were going, and what they had done and were doing seemed all to have been worked out within their own secret minds beforehand, in all those afternoons and nights of yearning towards one another, of half-aware waiting.

They went into Chris's room—and there they were, like his dreams, in his room, in that isolated, cut-off wing of the large house, no one else in the house, the tenants away at the University and the Landlady away somewhere; and he locked the door as in his dreams. It was mid-afternoon and already the darkening had begun, in the late winter way the days go. They were in each other's full embrace, naked in the bed where he had so often dreamed of this embrace, two bodies stretched long together touching everywhere; and he took from her and gave to her what they had only dared in the Park.

How long they stayed in the room, they could not remember, two or three days and nights. They loved each other out of the wordlessness with which they had come together into a wordlessness beyond any each of them had ever known; they spoke all other ways. At the end of this breathless and magical time they had given up everything in the living world for each other and taken it all back again, through each other. They began to talk. She told him that she had known that he was a kind of fugitive and that she wanted to give him sanctuary and heal him there. He learned that she was an orphan and had been brought up by an aunt and uncle out in the country east of the city. She was eighteen and had been very lonely.

He did not need to tell her of his loneliness. They knew, then, that they would make a life together, belonging, now, as they did to each other. There was some deep work they had to do together. They began to try to find a place to live where they could protect each other from the suspicions of men which seemed to them to want to destroy love wherever it could be found. They had to find a place to take their love life, to protect it and to defend it—for have you noticed the hostility of the world towards lovers? An odd thing—yet the world was made for two people only and it reveals itself fully only to two people, no more. They had in their minds an asylum to look for.

On their walks—Stella had returned to her room for appearance's sake—they met in the Park—they saw one day this large, unreal house that rose in the distance, across the city, whose gabled roofs emerged from the mist below like tents. Every day they watched this mysterious house—where was it?—that seemed to rise higher and higher above the city like a mirage or a vision. They decided to find it.

When they found it, what they saw was an abandoned handsome dwelling on a knoll by the side of the wide river. Its color was a delicate raspberry and its many windows were deep blue and carmine glass. There were four gables, each with little tentlike roofs, and over these rose a grand tented gable whose precious windows shone like jewels. They noticed that some preparation was in hand for destruction all around the magnificent house; and standing hand in hand on the ridge of the hill upon which the house sat, they saw evidence, already, of beginning destruction of smaller houses at the foot of the rise. There was the beginning of what would be something like a moat between the hill on which the house stood and the wide level land on one side of it. It was darkening, but they struggled across the moat and up the side of the torn hill to the house. They knocked but no one answered. They tried the door and were surprised to find it unlocked. They stepped into the enchanted country of this house which was to become theirs, stolen and unbeknownst to anyone. That night, near midnight, Stella and Chris moved into the stolen house, their sanctuary.

They chose the high turret to live in. It was round, of finial shape, full of windows, those on the river's side giving out upon the broad waters which vanished into a mysterious cavern made by two high foothills and filled with mist. On the opposite side were windows through which they could watch the mysterious work that was to go on, on the city's side. And through the eastern windows shone the erect head of the towering mountain. All below them were the three silent floors of the enormous house where the delicate life of a nonhuman world lived and went its unseen way. They did not interfere, Stella and Chris. They began their secret and stolen life together.

They began to establish their workdays of love, and their sensual nights were too beautiful and too terrible to be told. They lost their loneliness upon each other, here where it seemed they had rescued each other from that raging torrent of loneliness in which each of them was drowning: they had caught hold of each other and pulled each other up safe and rescued to this high, secure landing, and here they would, day by day, restore each other by love and by love's work.

The round room was their workroom, and in it love and work were the same. It was furnished, in the center of the room and around which all the life of the room lived, with a wide bed, this room of love, where they slept naked, ate together, had their conversations. It was the world of flesh and instinct, the bed-center of the lovers' world, it was a place of the blood and the love-cry, where they were leading each other to their beginnings and there to save each other and to heal each other. They cooked their meals together, ate together, washed themselves here in this room of love. Two people living together in love and making a way of life out of love is the ordering of the world.

Their workday of love was one of ferryings and crossings from shore to shore, island to island, of perceptions into death—it was the place of that death whose only relation is to life and dying out of life, and all their work was to remind them of their beginnings and to lead them to their beginnings out of their manifold deaths.

It was this marvelous, mortal love, their work at hand, with which they were obsessed and which was their only reality. They ate, slept, made love around it and through it. This work was related to and drew upon and into itself all life, for it existed in terms of human life and human life in terms of it. Can you see what they had rescued from the chaos of the world and were saving back in this round room of love, what had gone into such bad ways and had lost true mind of itself? Imagine their room in which their love was the living object, created by them and out of their own substance, to which they related the human world and through which they loved it. Who dare enter this room except to be disturbed by it? Yet it duplicated the great world beyond these two lovers, in its disorder and in its ferocity, that world through which we all move daily and some of us without fear, though not all of us. But what was the difference? There is *style* in the great world, a stylized manner of behavior which protects us, glides us through unharmed, just as in the work of many lovers who stylize themselves safely through their own spiritual disorder without being touched by it or without touching it to bring it to any suffering order. There was no style in this workroom but the style of the honest lover in possession of his Self or struggling to possess it and to give it away.

Yet in company with the doubts and anxieties and terrors of this revelation of their own Self's vision in love moved the dark brotherhood of murderer doubts and suspicions of Self; and there advanced upon my two lovers, Stella and Chris, in the fields of love, these assassins, the betrayals and self-slaughtering instincts of Cain. For deep and daring love leads lovers back through the ancestry of Love. Every day they had to face their legacy, and within this the failure of every man, the giant human failure, and bear mercy and charity and hold their belief in the power of repair. Can you see what their hard work was in that room of love? Facing this, their work was more than "self-expression," it was the image and the shape of one human being searching through every human being in himself for a finding of common truth. The revelations that came to them through this work were sometimes too terrifying to bear, they thought, finding that old first family living on exiled, in their loins; but they loved each other through these visions of despair and doom. This is the only way I can describe the love life of Stella and Chris, where their love life *really* lived. There is all that other to tell about, all that heaven and hell, that bliss and thrill and the hot devilment of lips and hands and of those magnificent instruments between the thighs, all of which would help me speak of love and to celebrate it. I can so beautifully imagine it, in my style of fancying, these two lying glued together as though their bodies had worked fiercely together to produce, out of themselves, a substance that would weld an architecture of flesh out of their two bodies, a dwelling of flesh in which they could live together, as insects built their dwellings . . . and how they had to tear apart this construction of flesh each time they rose to depart from this ancient smithy of the bed. We *are* beings of flesh, we must admit it; and if we were beings merely of stone and stone could tell, then the story of the building of magnificent edifices would only take us back to the quarry where the stone lay yearning in the earth, and to the *quarrying* of it, and to all the difficult inspired use of it in the building, as well as to the description and the praise of the finished wonder of great beauty. The materials and the labor that build our dwelling places are beautiful *in themselves,* and go way back to the beginning, to the stone that lay growing and hardening and waiting in the darkness, and to the raising of it, to the laying of stone upon stone, to the mortar that seals it and the hand that touches it to shape.

In their room were dead flowers from another day, dead leaves, broken candlesticks, Chris's trunk for a table, suitcases under the bed, the golden bed looking as if they had tried to destroy it, cigarette ends, ashes, a golden lamp, the disorder of passion. But in the center of the room and from which all its life and chaos emanated was the shining, quiet simplicity of the order of light they made, if only for moments, like a match struck, and out of the animal darkness in themselves and some God in the room. There were stains of food and drink, tears and sperm. And when they went to the windows there clashed, beyond, the howling, bristling mob of the world: collectors of delinquent bills knocking at the doors, money-hounds, makers of war, killers, thieves, beggars, fringers, imitators, the chic: the eternal daily human traffic at their windows. Yet they knew that they, too, were among the crowd, outside their own windows, that they were on both sides of their windows: outside: their own enemy to order come to remind them of their brotherhood; inside: two people together saving back, like thieves, a stolen redemption. I remind you of their look, as they faced their work and the world in their round room.

In the evenings, under the stars, they would row on the river in the little boat they found in the boathouse. They would be wan and languid and somehow sad, sometimes, from all their work in the room; but often, even like that, they would fall together in their love again, and this was often the most beautiful and most terrifying love of all. Afterwards, they floated along in the little shell of the boat, exhausted and drained by the work of love. Sometimes when the boat was drifting towards the other side of the river, Chris would change its course and turn it back. Stella sometimes wanted to cross to the other side, but Chris would say, "This is our side; over there is not for us."

Then they began to row across the moat from the house to the mainland, at night, tie up the little boat and walk into the city for their necessities. When they came down into the world, onto the street, they clung to each other to find each other real and no fantasy, and, gladdened by that, they passed through the crowds they had watched through their high and secret windows in the tower. They felt the disorder around them and the antipathy towards them, for they were strangers. They must have looked so very beautiful, so beautiful that people who saw them feared them, and, fearing them, desired them—in the way that desire wishes to destroy. Being so vulnerable and feeling themselves so beautiful, they knew they had to defend themselves and protect each other, for any stranger on the street might raise a brute arm to threaten to destroy them. Why should the act of love, of the creation of beauty, provoke violence and fear and this half-Cain in men? We speak of how love purifies and chastens and spiritualizes, but we must be reminded that it demonizes, as well. If you could have seen those faces on the street you would have recognized this truth of which I speak: these two seemed to have been fired in some kiln: that is what their room was, a kiln where their work had been to *fire* each other. Their lips showed it: Chris's pale and swollen lip-flesh showed it had been touched and retouched until it was quick and sensitive of itself, the corona of his lips was edged with moisture and a slippery road for the tip of a finger to slide upon; and in his eyes was such a bright and burning look; there was that warm, rubbery, moist look about him that the observer feels he can taste in some lovers. And upon Stella's face was that labial look and a look of having been brought to abundance. Chris and Stella had loved each other into something beautiful and dangerous, they disturbed the streets they walked in; they had brought down into the city a magnificent animal heritage which belonged to all the inhabitants of that city and which they had been suffering through as though it were something terrible and marvelous happening to the city and not *in* the city but *above* it, up over it.

Now my tale of these two lovers might seem to you to be about how love—which ought to make a "community of men"—alienates lovers from their society even as criminals are. But has it not been shown to you by the history of human love that our great lovers have been crucified victims, sacrificed to the broad, general enlightenment of the ways of the human heart? Great lovers suffer for us all, and by their heights and depths of bliss and agony; for they live out our dreadful legend of sacrifice and yielding and loss that wins back over and over again what is lost. The work of lovers does not "save" them, it kills them, slowly, time after time, so that lovers are working towards their death, which is their life, facing all our darkness and redeeming it to light. I speak of a grand and tragic love, and no other. After all, I am Curran.

For a long time the machines below the house had lain in the mud like sleeping monsters that might wake—and destroy the house. One morning, the lovers heard their noises, and sure enough they looked down to see that a large crew of workmen had arrived and were already at work. They began to dig and chew, eating out the ground below the house so that the house rose higher and higher and seemed to recoil further and further from the city and the destroyers. The lovers were more and more cut off from the world outside, and the surrounding land became more and more wasted and barren. But they had given each other this home, this base and center of reference where all things would come to order, to which they could relate everything that happened to them, even this destruction below; and they began to see its meaning.

Now Chris had gone simple, back to his beginnings, the way he once had been, so long ago, and the only way he could live. "For two years I have not been anything but something running and panting and wanting to die, and killing. Now I have fallen back, to my beginning, and there I will stay, where I have found you and where I will go with you." Stella blessed him. They had so much to tell each other. They talked and talked, for the first time they knew what all their conversations in the world had been about. The sweetness of their dialogues permeated the air of their round room, and finally it seemed they had spoken of all things men had ever spoken about, together, touching everything dear and tender and fearful, and that they had brought it all into this room, this sanctuary, to protect and to keep it.

But the destruction below was coming closer and closer, and its approach increased their sense of limit, as though they were soon to die. They were ready, now, to die, having this life to die out of. Soon the destroyers would be upon them. When they went down into the city they listened to conversations to try to overhear what the object of the destruction was, whether it was the house. They asked questions when they could, but men only spoke vaguely of the "construction east of town."

Finally, one night in a little restaurant where they sat, they heard men speaking of the Superhighway to be built east of town and they heard them speak of razing the house they worked in. The house was condemned and its life was short. Now they knew the end was near, the destroyers would be at the door and windows, then inside the house, and then they would bring it down to ruin, with all that the lovers had created and kept alive within it. But the destroyers would never know. Chris and Stella would never let them discover it . . . they would destroy what they did not even know they had destroyed and destroy it at its work. The lovers' days of work were numbered.

Chris and Stella returned to the house and, in the room again, they knew that it did not matter, that their work would go on as though no killer or enemy were at the door and that they would be destroyed, finally, in the act of their work, in the act of love. They went on, serenely and without fear. For some time they had known that Stella was going to have a child.

But someone else began to live in the room with them, now. One day Chris saw, suddenly, in one of the windows towards the city the shape of a figure ascending a flagpole on one of the city's highest buildings. The day he was raised was a strange unreal day for the lovers, for they had quarreled for the first time, an idiot quarrel rising out of things they had not talked about but had kept within themselves, and these reserved thoughts and fantasies, having to do with jealousies and fears which all lovers know, had fermented without their knowing it into these poisonous vapors of sudden ferocity. They were amazed, during the conflict and afterwards, when each of them was so hurt and humiliated, cowering alone in his corner, that they could be so savage towards each other, as though they could hate each other, as though, suddenly, they were murderous enemies. So Stella and Chris found that it was not only their magnificent love for each other which they had daily to try to understand, their daily work in the room, but their possible hatred. It was on this day, then, after their quarrel when they were wounded by each other and withdrawn into their corners, that the flagpole sitter was raised, as though their abuse of love had elevated him, to remind them. When Chris spied the figure suddenly, as he sat alone, the whole quarrel was over and he and Stella joined each other, again, at the window.

There they saw the flagpole sitter. They had bought binoculars, and through them they saw this figure.

"He is such a little man," Stella said.

"That's because he's huddled over," Chris answered.

The flagpole sitter began to obsess the lovers. They watched him both day and night so that it finally seemed he had come into their room, living with them and participating in the work they did. Once they saw him looking at them through his glasses, for he had seen them, too. They were discovered! Now the flagpole sitter was the only living person in the wide world who knew them and who knew where they were.

They gave him a name. It was Marvello. Sometimes, in the deep of night, Chris would rise and go to the window and call out "Marvello! Marvello!"; and it seemed Marvello could hear his call and answer him and that they were having a conversation, although Chris could not tell clearly what it was about. It was like the speakings and listenings in music, but these conversations seemed, or *felt*, to be about life and death, about saving and losing, about love.

Yet Marvello gave them a sense of themselves, Stella and Chris, and at first they felt this good. He gave them a feeling of pride in their work, a sense of their animal prowess, a regarding of their own self's beauty; and once they let him watch them make love and felt for the first time a terrifying and marvelous sensation: that they had loved each other *through* him, and more—that he had *participated*. Their love, through such a great new sense of itself, became so aggrandized that it led them into ways they had never dreamt were open to them, believing that they had traveled all roads to it. They began to ask questions of themselves, and then of each other. Were they evil or divine? Was Marvello mocking and betraying their work or was he supporting and blessing it? They became suspicious of each other. "You are hiding something from me," Stella would say to Chris.

"No," Chris would answer, darkly.

"Then why are you so strange?"

"It is Marvello," Chris said, disturbed.

One night Stella said to Chris, "When the child comes it will be Marvello's." Chris trembled. Now it seemed that Marvello had been with them all the time, through all their work and all their stolen life.

The destruction below continued, and at the darkest times it had seemed to be the work of Marvello. Again, and in the face of Marvello and all he had brought to them, Stella and Chris had to make the choice. It was the crucial time, for not only were the men and machines so near the house that their faces, which seemed to resemble each other, could be clearly seen, but Stella could feel the child struggling to be born. They would stay in the room and vanish, all three, with the house.

All day the explosions were so violent and so near that the room rumbled and shuddered. The quakes of the blasts were bringing the child from Stella. Chris helped her into their bed in the afternoon, and it seemed the whole earth was heaving to help Stella free the child from her body. Through the window Chris watched the whole city that seemed to shiver with the explosions, and he saw Marvello crouched upon the flagpole and folded into himself in a natal shape. Would the blasts bring him down, was he in danger of falling? He seemed to be clutching on to himself, having nothing else to hold to, to stay himself, but Chris watched his body tremble with the quakes, and the flagpole swayed like a mast in a storm.

That night the child was born and Chris delivered it, with the help, he knew, of Marvello. Stella lay very weak and near death, Chris feared; but he put the child in the crook of her arm against her tired body in their bed. She looked at Chris and said, "We will call the baby Marvello," and at that moment they heard a tumult in the city.

Chris went to the window and saw searchlights playing over a mob at the foot of the flagpole where Marvello sat and there were lights fixed on the top of the pole where there was nobody. Then Chris heard the cries, first softly so that he thought he imagined what they cried out, but then the cries grew louder and louder and they came into the room and reverberated through all the room, *"Marvello has fallen!"*

Stella and Chris were silent, knowing they had lost something. So the blasts of the destroyers had dislodged Marvello, they had thrown him down. As Chris looked again through the window he saw that the searchlights were playing upon the river which ran by the building where Marvello's flagpole was, and he said to Stella, "He has fallen into the river."

All night Chris lay by Stella's side, the child between them. Stella was deathly ill, the birth of the child had been so hard. Through the long night, Chris whispered out over and over again, "Marvello, come over to us, cross over to Stella and me and our child, for we need you, Marvello!"

In the morning Stella was very low and Chris fed the child at her breast. Below, the destroyers were at the very door of the house, and when Chris looked down at them through the binoculars he saw that they had the faces of all those he had harmed in love. This was the day of destruction. "Let them come," he said to himself, "we will all three die together in this our only world, in the home we have made and kept against so much."

They were in the house now, on the first floor, and Chris heard the crashing of walls as if a windstorm were in the rooms. Quickly he heard them move to the second floor, their methods were so adept and powerful; and then he heard footsteps of those coming up the stairs who would lay the dynamite at the door. They did not know what they were about to destroy, and they would never know.

Chris watched Stella losing her last breath, and as he heard the hands at the door of the round room of love—he knew what they were leaving there—he saw her, as he held her in his arms and child on her breast, die away. He covered her with the blanket they had lain under so many times, laid the child against her side and stretched his body close against them both. Then he drew the blanket over the family. "Let them come, Stella," he whispered, "we are ready"; and he folded his body around her body and the baby's, in their bed. And then the great, empty house collapsed with one blast.

In the middle of the river, sitting in a little boat, was a figure watching. He may have been the Overseer or the Supervisor; but he saw the house cave in, heard the loud roar of its crumbling, saw it vanish for a moment in dust and smoke; and then, when the dust had cleared, there was no longer any sign of it. The figure in the boat would wait until the destroyers, who had done such a good and thorough job, had left; and before they would come back to clear away the rubble so completely that in a few years people would never have known a house had stood there, he would search the ruins and watch the shore for some sign and shape of the life he alone had witnessed and watched in that high room, and across such a great distance, to see if it meant what he had imagined it to mean. Then, when he could salvage what gave itself up to the boat and the crossing, what might be so valuable for a long time to come, he would row the boat across the wide water, crossing to that other country with his cargo.

But the rescuer in the boat had to wait a little longer for his passenger, though his passenger was visible, now, wandering up and down the shore by the ruins, in the company of another, a shadow, perhaps—but there were two and the rescuer was waiting only for one. His passenger would have to make a final choice, here on the edge of the boundary that divided the two countries; and the rescuer would have to wait for that.

What I mean to tell is that the figure on the shore, so close to yielding to the passage, had yet to yield, by preparing himself through giving up, courageously sacrificing, to my healing and deliverance of him. Then he would cross to the other side and begin again. I am trying to tell it for him, who, being as he was—the kind of person who would write down what I had read in his notebook—could not tell it any other way except through his own slanting way. I was measuring the worth and validity of what had happened to him, what he had seen—and not seen—, by the depth of his understanding of what had happened to him, and hoping to add my own to his. I was serving him this way, I hoped, as I helped him to heal, to prepare himself. I read the last notation in his record—and worked the loom in the area of his loins—

IV

the dangerous archipelago
(THE PATIENT'S NOTEBOOK)

The act was a marvel. It was one of perfect grace and balance
and imperiled order. The bodies of The Three were clothed
entirely in the purest white garments like another layer of their
skin and tight as their own flesh, though they seemed somehow
beyond nudity. The muscles of the two men, and particularly
those of Marvello, who was powerful yet lithe, and the gentle
liquid quiver of their buttocks, swelled and sank and tightened
with the erotic grace of male passion. Their thighs and loins and
bellies surrounded, as if to insulate it, that dangerous engine
whose language The Act seemed to be, the hub and the shaft
which turned the wheel of this marvelous machinery.

The two men drew near each other upon the wire in a gradually increasing ferocity of pressing, their torsos hunching and
relaxing and hunching again as they balanced themselves aloft;
and then the girl, a crystal and stellar creature, would slide
down between them, delicately fitting as the blade of a sword;
and together, in an overwhelmingly exciting climax, the two
young men would fit against her almost as if they were molding
themselves around her voluptuous form—it was marvelous the
way their bodies fitted into one magnificent white body of
flesh—and moved, like a machine, to lift her up as though they
had ejected her from the cleaving opening between their one
body which their two bodies had made. For a moment, then, she
had slipped from above where she perched on a rod, which both
of them held, into the cove of their two bodies, had merged into
their bodies so that what one saw was one male-female body, a

dazzlingly sensual androgynous being; and in another moment, the single androgyne was writhing and hunching and flexing, and in the next, the female part of this momentarily created being was thrust upward out of them as though having been suddenly created out of that moment of fierce and turbulent work and borne into the world of air above them. She, as if newly created and pure as that, hovered in the air above the two men, quivering and beatified; and then down into the erotic male machine she slid again. What was it we were watching? Something we almost dared not look upon, yet a sight from which we could not turn our eyes. It was clear that The Three existed in a violently sensual relationship, yet what we saw was the spiritual manifestation of it. It was the silence of it all that thrilled and terrified us, this act of "Gli Maravigliosi," "The Marvelous Ones" in the Roman Carnival.

The Three flexed and shimmered in a pale moss-blue light that was cast upon them from somewhere above; their act was an engine of all order and exquisitely wrought relationships; and when they were still, in the shape they finally made and held, their fury and energy spent—how long? it seemed timeless—there was a residual quality of purity, of peace, of chastity about them. It was a marvel to behold. Outside, in the stalls of the sideshows were the huge beasts, the monsters and the misshapen, and on the platforms were the dishonest bodies of mountebanks; and beyond these the disorder of the town; and farther beyond, the chaos of the human world. But here, under this pale light in this tent within a tent, was the beautiful shape of order wrought through sensual work. These three seemed to have been struggling not only *with* the bodies of each other—for this is what they had to work with towards that ultimate *bodiless* shape they achieved, so that it was, finally, the shape of an *idea*—but *against* the bodies of each other, in some tension, some resistance. Yet through it all they came to this serene shape of clean, of purified order. Something unclean was purified in us who watched, something imperfect was made, for the moment of watching, flawless: we would hold the memory of this to go by, if we could keep to it, outside this tent, in the sideshows where we watched the twistings and grovelings of animals and freaks, in the town and beyond in the world where we struggled within ourselves and in the daily world. One could not destroy the vision of the *gesture* of The Three, though he could not describe the shape of the gesture—was it that of a cross, the strong Marvello as the beam and the young man and young woman as the slender crosspieces, for at the overwhelming climax, in the shape they finally made and held so timelessly, Marvello held the two aloft. Was it the shape of a weathervane as the two birdlike creatures turned in the air around the swiveling cock-body of Marvello; was it a finial shape on the top of a stunning tower of a human body? There was no describing it. Through my American mind kept running the little nursery rhyme *This is the house that Jack built.* But the gesture of this made shape was put into the minds of all onlookers, as if under a small glass dome, where it would hang, like the gesture itself, to pacify to order or torment to disorder.

Afterwards, spent and quietened and relieved of some tension, of some yearning and craving within ourselves, we tried to buy photographs of the Marvelous Ones to keep as a reminder; but there were none to be had, nor had any ever been made, we came to understand. In fact, the audience was searched for cameras before the performance began. There was to be no recording of this indescribable gesture but that which no man could prohibit, and many wished they could, of the senses. That, I knew, was the truth of The Three, that they had created for us the kind of experience that lives in one's senses. How many live in our loins, in our eyes, in our ears and lips! But many agents could destroy this sensual recording or mutilate it beyond recognition: the devilish mirrors within ourselves that distort into pantomime and caricature, that betrayal of the sense, that sensual deception we all use so well to wither away what lives in our senses, the betrayal of the gesture. Yet one knew that the spirit, honest and pure and just, holds the rod and walks the wire upon which the flesh performs, the spirit's work. I knew that we all only wanted and searched for something to be true to, some small sensual image which our minds could hold like a hand or an object, through which we could be true to the spiritual choices we had made and struggled to keep; and as something through which we could love our human world and, particularly, the beloved we would, each of us, one day find and keep to and do our work with, perilously balancing.

When the act of The Three was finished, when it vanished—or, really, when it was broken and destroyed as if it had been a delicate and ephemeral object of ice-blue glass melted away by a hot flame—a little tent fell and covered them where they remained until the crowd had left the larger tent under which The Three had performed.

—Rome, 19–

The sight of The Three was a deep experience of my life which I had not at all anticipated, having come to the little Carnival to amuse myself or really to distract myself from myself—I had been devouring myself in my room, trying to understand my afflicted state of mind which accompanied my temporary physical affliction: a crippled leg resulting from a severe fall in Rome several weeks back. I was battling the eventual necessity of an operation on the bone, which I had injured and kept hoping would repair itself with the help of my own treatment. To be afflicted in Rome is to be unhappy and alienated from the quick and lusty life of the streets; and the ruins, if one stands among them lame, persecute one—not to mention the mockery of the lovely people of the fountains. This profound experience, then, was a beginning for me, the kind that marks a start after long long halting and waiting. Perhaps it was because of my own crippledness that the agile movements of The Three moved me so. Why was it that I did not feel mocked by these? But no, it was more than that, certainly. What I had seen involved, was related to, I knew clearly now, my *whole* search, spiritual and sensual: someone, some idea to work with towards a final simple shape of order, through danger.

As I hobbled away from the performance that night, The Act grew and grew in my memory. It became, somehow, what had begun as an overwhelming sensual experience that had made me feel, I must confess, desire at the very quick of my fingernails and at the roots of my hair, an act of Heroes, an expression of human dignity in which honor was somehow involved, and compassion. I felt that some majestical danger was lurking there within The Act, as though The Act were a test of each of The Marvelous Ones and none could fail the other, for one failure would be a total failure; and that something would be lost, something precious and permanent, like the loss of a limb, if The Three failed. How could I return to my room where a cripple lived, where I lived halted? And when, when would my injury heal and my own spirit, so wounded, too, by my physical wound? Now The Act had assured me that I was right and that its way, the way of its work, was the human way towards danger and towards the curing of that affliction which I suffered. We, ourselves, are both the patient and the nurse; we are that fusion of subject and object.

For I had walked, fugitive, out of this room of giant disorder, as though Cain had lived there, where the weight of my secret life was heavy as fallen stone and nothing, nothing would rise

out of it, or who would raise it again; though I knew the fragility
of my violence and the delicacy of my ferocity. My life now was
filled and haunted with the sense of enormous objects falling,
like buildings into street, bridges into rivers and statues into
plazas, until I had stumbled onto this vision of The Marvelous
Ones and all had been ended with the sense of fragile flights and
glimmers of small risings and flutterings. My room was the living
place of an injured man: it seemed a place of physical violence.
There were broken things there because I had stumbled often—
in the night when I would rise, sleepless and restless and tormented by my half-dreams; furniture and objects were in disar-
ray because I could not very well help myself and there was no
one to tend to me—no one ever entered my room, I have such a
feeling about the privacy of my own dwelling place (perhaps
there was the abiding guilt there, too, of my fantasies which, I
felt, inhabitated the room with me as though I had smuggled
companions there): one would have thought some murder had
occurred there and that the murdered lived on at the scene of it,
with the murderer, in that room of affliction. The Landlady,
one of those "interesting" women the foreigner is accustomed to
meeting and whose accent leads him to believe, for a while, that
she is speaking great wisdom, and so laconically, of the heart
and the flesh—the Landlady came occasionally to the door with
a hot water bottle when she heard me groaning at midnight with
the pain in my throbbing and swollen joint; but I would not take
it, so as not to be in any way beholden to her and to keep my
place a secret place. And one of the tenants, I learned when she
knocked at my door one night, was a British Physiotherapist
who offered to show me exercises and manipulations to pacify
the pain, but I refused her help, too. Somehow, I had to understand my wound and live with it, upon its own terms, in a secret
place as though it were a private theater of war, and try to cure
it myself. I was obsessed with this task and felt it a very personal, a very secret task of my own.

When I left the performance of The Three, then, I knew I
could not return to that room. Where was I to go? If only there
were a friend, somewhere in this city who, like myself, was
sitting alone in his room and who would welcome me when I
knocked at his door and to whom I could tell all that had
happened to me. But there was no one. This was my own fault
because I had alienated all the amicable overtures of strangers
as soon as I had seen signs of friendliness in them, urged by
something in me to be alone with my animal wound and my

burden until I could understand it myself and rehabilitate it, alone.

After that indescribable vision of The Three, there seemed no world outside to go into, no buildings or streets, only the memory of the tent within the tent, and within the small tent the hanging shape of The Marvelous Ones as though it were a crystalline pendant of fragile ice. I thought, I cannot bear the image of The Three, I will try to destroy the image of this marvel in my memory; I will debase it; I will go to the world of violence I know so well, having come from it to see this vision tonight.

But why? I asked myself, in that miserable dialogue with myself that had gone on so long. Could it be that I have fallen in love with The Three? At that thought I was incensed by the wildest passion for them as I struggled along in the dark street. I felt the same desire, again, that I had felt when I watched The Act in the tent. It was a desire to make a shape, like these, of beautiful and purified order, that it might influence others as it had me, hurl them into that fierce distress out of which they had to make a choice, and in such danger: this lust, for it was that, to make a spiritual shape to these ends, invaded me through my veins and loins. I felt driven to find The Three tonight, at once, for now I knew that I desired them and it was as though I wished to possess them in the flesh, who had so moved my spirit. At that moment, as I turned around and began to walk toward the tent again, the whole long and revolutionary experience of which I am to tell you began.

As I hobbled back towards the tent, driven with my uncontrollable passion to find The Three, I asked myself, "But which should I call for?" I could not answer that. At the door of the tent, I called out "Hello-o-o!"; and Marvello appeared.

I saw that he was old, that he looked like a dying and withering man! He looked at me fiercely.

I uttered the banal and dishonest words people use at the doors of theater dressing rooms or on the telephone, "I am sorry to intrude, but . . ."; and I had no more to say.

"Come in . . . ," was all Marvello said.

In the tent, which was drab, I saw the other two. The girl, Maria, was sullen and unhappy looking, and the young man, Cario, looked beautifully disturbed and harried. How different The Three seemed! They were three troubled people, that was all I could feel. Had I come at the wrong moment, had something gone wrong among them, had they quarreled or lost something or received bad news? I sat down. Maria and Cario looked at me suspiciously, then they went into a farther room. Marvello said to me, kindly yet withdrawn,

"If you will wait here until I change my clothes, I'll speak with you." I dropped my head and watched him as he left the room. I wanted to run, to vanish. What had I done? What would I say, I who had uttered nothing but the daily requests of clerks and waiters for so many months.

In a while, Marvello returned and suggested that we go elsewhere "where we could talk." "The walk will do us good," he said, ignoring my lame leg and my cane.

"But . . ." I said, gesturing towards my leg; and he answered severely,

"You can walk. As we talk you will forget your infirmity."

We left the tent and began to walk towards the city, very slowly. There was a long time of silence. Finally Marvello asked me, "What is it you wish to say to me?"

I was silent. As we walked it began to rain lightly, and the lights of the town we were approaching glimmered in it like sunlit dandelions. Suddenly Marvello began to talk, as though we had been having a long conversation which had been only momentarily interrupted.

"Sometimes, as I hold them, they seem to me to be the whole world, my burden; sometimes I die, holding them up; and who knows this? What we do is one thing, and that is what is seen by those who watch us; but the idea of what we do, our secret, is the reality of what we do. I must forever keep before myself, in my mind, the sense of what I am doing. . . ."

I listened.

"But if I could tell someone the marvelous experience of holding them aloft! They are in love with each other, but only when I support them . . . they keep wanting to stay longer in the air, until I think one day my strength, so weakened—for look at me, how tired and used I am—one day I might not be able to support them any longer, and let them fall. But they keep whispering down to me, 'Longer! longer, Marvello!' until I can hardly bear it. For you see, my listener, their love survives in me; I am a carrier; I *bear* love, I support love. In The Act, I become a figure in which and through which people love one another, without fear, whom and what they cannot love in life outside The Act. I live off their love, which exists only through me. But oh I long for someone of my own, to have in the tent and outside the tent. Yet if I desert them, they fall and will destroy each other. What am I to do? I grow old fast, yet I am a young man. I am unused, except in this magnificent way. There is my body . . . my nature. I tell myself that I exist to support these two, to be the living image through which their magnificent love can flourish and bring beauty to so many . . . and I enlarge it to mean that I am, after my destiny, meant to be the agent of love, lonely myself; that I must forget self, surrender self to become nature through this suffering, this losing of self. Do you see my living paradox? Can an Idea become nature? a man?

"We have no life together or apart outside The Act. We are all separate though we are together constantly, but we are full of rancor and simmering animosities and antipathies—something in us all is wounded then. But this vanishes when we go into The Act, and then what is wounded is healed within us, within our solitary secret tent that covers us before we appear; and it, the . . . *ugliness* . . . begins again after The Act, the moment the tent falls around us.

"We three wanted a community of love, as we thought of it. But desiring each other and living through each other, there is no 'community' possible until each of us cures himself through the *whole* love of another; and I seek that. That will be my beginning . . . out of a destruction. The moment of destruction is coming, it is ahead; and I dread it, it will be terrible to behold—but out of it will come the rescue I wait for."

I listened.

"But we three are in a despicable conspiracy, for each of us can bring the others to the fullest ordering of himself, and so can each of us bring the other, and all of us through him, to destruction: we all, the three of us, have this double power. I must tell you," Marvello said, stopping in the rain for a moment and looking me again straight in the eye, "that when I found you standing terrible at the door of our tent, I was afraid for a moment, for you looked like Satan or like Death—*my* Death come for me—the dangerousness of you. When I saw that you dragged one leg, I stepped back from you, if you will remember, with that instinctive repulsion I have for the lamed, the one secret fear of aerialists, who have a superstition that Death comes for them in the shape of a lame figure. When I asked you to come in, I was still not sure of you, whether you were a thief or a murderer, you had such a delicate criminal look. But when you looked up at me and said . . . nothing . . . I could not turn you out."

I listened.

"I wanted to show them a good life, for I looked for that, too. But you see *they* make it possible for me to show them a 'good life'; so you can see how love, so simple, can bring to us the good whole human life through ourselves, out of ourselves, as though we brought it to ourselves, what we could never have brought to ourselves alone and in our misery of half-life and no love. Others lead us to ourselves, as though to this someone, the right one. The right one touches us and we open up ourselves, but because he touched us, because he opened our door. Maria and Cario and I have done this for each other, it is a work of love, The Act; and it could never be a beautiful thing to see without love in it. Yet, I cannot be wholly of the air or of the ground. For a life wholly of either leads only to suffering and despair and destruction . . . even of self. It is time to break this—but how?—which has brought me to a new self-knowledge; it is time to pass on through it to an undisguised and new self. I wait for that . . ."

I had come to speak to Marvello, to tell him, I hoped, everything. But I had only listened while he spoke, as though he had never spoken to anyone in his life. And where I had thought to find a serene idol into whom I could pour all my questions, so unanswerable and so meaningless, and receive from him answers and meanings, I found, it seemed to me at the moment, a man obsessed with his own paradox, laboring with his secret travail, who miraculously managed to bring into being a living shape of order and beauty which influenced me towards it. As this thought filled me with despair and vitiated what I thought was my last hope, I heard Marvello murmuring,

"There are those among the admirers of The Act who call us The Three Angels—and there are our enemies who name us The Three Fiends. Both admirer and enemy are right. How bitter to know that perhaps the only way to know and to find our Angel is by surrendering to the Fiend."

If Marvello turned later, and suddenly, to look in my face, he did not see it, for at the turning of a street I left him, going on and on in the inner speech of a lonely man in the capture of an idea of himself. I went on away, dragging my lame leg through the rain and into the blindness of the winter midnight towards my dreadful room, thinking that there is no progress except the inner progress of the spirit and the human soul—the way a man shapes his own life by the choices he makes, and the conflicts of these choices with the choices of the society he lives in: whether to imitate the style of his society or to oppose it.

And then, in my room, I was sure I understood the machinery within Marvello that raised and held aloft the two beautiful young people in their purity, in their splendor. In creating his masterpiece, Marvello had created, as well, the flaw in it; and now I saw that part of his task as creator was to discover means of overcoming the flaws which were in his own making. And now, all in the room was the sense of something ended. A balance was struggling, a shape from outside, in the world, and inside, in a dream, was at work. There is a link, I knew now, between the happenings of the daily world and the dreaming mind that holds its hidden images. We cannot believe how all things work together towards some ultimate clear meaning, we cannot believe. Human life is at once in a conspiracy of incidents and images to lead us to a beginning again. There is the constant gentle and steadfast urging of the small loyal friendliness, the pure benevolence of some little Beginningness that lies waiting in us all to be taken up like a rescued lover and lead us to a human courage and a human meaning: love, human life. The rest is death: murder (self or other), betrayal, violence and cruelty, vengeance and crimes of fear. But the little Beginningness is in all of us, waiting.

—Rome, 19–.

America, my wildwood, break your old wilderness back through me!

I write this down before me on a page of paper to remind myself that I am, by nature, pioneer. It is my instinct as it is my destiny to cut clear, to blaze free, as trail and clearing. For this, something keeps me rude and ground-minded and turns me from worn paths into thickets. This force of making clear, traversible, navigable, has borrowed my life's time for the labor and mission of handchopper, this force of taking to myself for my own and to make new what has always been living in the lasting world, is as primitive as forest and grass and thorn, and it is lent me like a good plain ax to hew with handlespit my own clearing out of the brambles where I find myself to be, discover myself to have arrived (through going my way), making use of the materials of that place to make it, like a bird its nest of local twigs and grass, and to consider what is given a divine generosity so that it be honest, authentic work, of a time real and inevitable, turned under a traveling man's hands, of humanity, product of mortality cut clean out of what was wild and grown over upon itself, does not die but flourishes up and grows over again, obscuring the work of the blazing hand. The instrument of clearing and blazing, the ax, is the enduring monument to the energy that used it, the indestructible, unrusting axhead lying in the wilderness.

I distrust all roads that do not crumble and are not over-thrown by grass and weed in the crevices between the stones; all bridges that never weaken and fall under washout of the water they cross. I tickle the tombs of Caesars with a blade of grass, and my own flesh.

The struggle to *rise*, to *climb*, to disencumber of this fragile net round us that holds us on the ground, this feeling of being held down, or of having stumbled down: the history of stumbled-down, fallen-down peoples, what there is to know and to help *up* in it, to help *rise up* from it: there, there.

The only times I have been free, that I have risen out of this net that briefly and miraculously fell away from me was in the act of love and in the act of work: one led me to the other.

I think I must have some instrument of marvels on me, trilling gladdest tidings, that it stands up for so much good and truth and is of such simple message: that there is no good or truth except in this mortal disaster of love that holds the heartbreak in it: that we go nowhere, only arrive, only come somewhere, and come again . . . and come again.

So I think I will go away, now; I think I will go, now, and find me a place of earth and unclothe myself and sink, naked and erotic, between the loamy thighs of earth, sowing down into dirt and cutting through shale and clay to a very bottomland, seeding in fountains as I clip down and down and down—this oh great glory of flesh of grass.

For I have had sad news, sad news at the American Express.

Depart Rome, 19–.

It was Recreation Hour and all the ambulatory patients were on the floor, either on crutches or in wheelchairs, the Wireless was booming with music, men were calling at each other, nurses were giggling and running about, patients with great white plaster legs were playing billiards on the huge table in the center of the room. Bobby was whirling about the floor in his little wheelchair and Lord Bottle was in the midst of a preachment we had heard so many times that we could all say it with him. The sun was sinking over the Channel, and tea was being brought around. Suddenly Chris roused out of his sleep, as if to have his tea, for the table had just progressed to his cot; and through his lips thickened and numbed from sleep he called my name "Cuhun . . ." as though he had said "Cain." I answered, Chris will you have some tea?, and handed him a cup.

"What have you been doing?" he asked me.

"Tending you," I said, "and waiting to get you on your feet. You've slept past the time when we put patients to the ground; and my guess is that at tomorrow's Recreation Hour we can start teaching you how to walk again."

"Do you think I have forgotten how to walk?" he asked.

"Operations on the leg rob the leg of its knowledge of mobility," I said, "and the patient literally has to be taught to walk again, as though the limb had forgotten its natural function. It won't take long, now."

Daily I walked Chris about the ward at Recreation Hour while the other patients called out cheers and encouragements to him; and within a week Chris was able to walk with a crutch, and several days later with a cane. We did not say much to each other, being the kind of strangers we were to each other. We knew each other somewhere else.

The day came for his release from the hospital; and Chris and I said good-bye. "There is a certain weather that will cause your injury to ache," I said to him. "Then you will limp." He thanked me for my care, but when the doctor came to say good-bye, Chris praised him abundantly for healing his leg, and I watched them walk away, Chris limping slightly, down the corridor together. I had kept the notebook for myself: my patient had gone but I had kept his idea which had become so much my own that I could not have returned it to him without yielding great portion of myself to him; and there was no separation possible, one from the other.

So much of myself had gone into Chris that I felt selfless when he was gone. I went to the hospital window and saw him wait at the landing as the boat tied up. Then I saw him board the boat, and I thought I saw someone come gladly to take his hand as though he had come for Chris. And as the boat moved away to cross the water to the other side, I was sure, now, that I saw Chris and the one who had met him standing beside one another on the prow of the boat, joined at last, as it went towards the other side. From there, they would take the ship towards . . . home.

VI

In the terrible absence of Chris, my object, I finished his tale—and ended the Record:

What had led him away brought him back: the image of the Flagpole Sitter. He returned to the town that now seemed to him only the territory of Shipwreck Kelley. It was the time of another war, but somehow this seemed a gayer war, it produced, astonishingly enough, a kind of abundance among people. It seemed a war that could be afforded and one that could be enjoyed.

The town was a city now, as he was a man, so that change disguised both. He took a room high up in a building on a busy street. Day and night he did no more than sit by his window, watching the life below, humped under his burden. Once he was free of it, he could use it, what hung upon him, what he carried.

As he watched through the window, his meeting again with all he had known before was dreamlike, for he saw familiar faces; and finally, one by one, everyone he had known before passed by below him. Even his parents came by—one day he saw two gray people pass and it was his mother and father, as though they were searching for him.

All below him lay the country of his beginnings. He had a pair of binoculars and through them he sought out and found right away the small wooden house where he was born and where he had lived with his mother and father until he had abandoned them, long years ago; and he saw the long backyard where so many scenes had followed each other like a moving picture of his own history. He saw the little pasture and the shed fallen to one side with age. All the backyards of small houses looked sad and still kept, like the parlors of these very houses where the members of families had once gathered on occasions that united them. He drew all he had known of his neighborhood within the round frame of the binoculars, and he saw it little changed outside except to look so very used and as though it were waiting for those who had left it to come back and bring it back to use, to what it had been, as though all that had been had a memory and a yearning of its own.

During the long days and nights of his self-internment in this high room, his observatory, he watched the life of the streets and the households below him, sometimes with his binoculars, sometimes with his naked eye. He saw how the crowds moved like herds, or convoys of boats, or like regiments, sometimes all in step. Had they forgotten Shipwreck Kelley? How desirable all humanity looked!—as though the time of the Flagpole Sitter had never happened to them. Had it, this company of people, all having gone through the years together, advancing or backsliding, burying and marrying, breeding and aging, made any progress? Would it do the same thing again? Since he cared so much, it was up to *him* to know. Had *he* made any progress? Would *he* do the same thing? Sometimes he would see for a moment a face or a body that would haunt him all night. He sat, removed like the limb of a body that passed below him, raised and removed to heal and to mend, having been wounded by himself, by his own body. As he watched them go by, he thought, in his loneliness, "Who woke up with him this morning, warm in the comfort of his arms and close against his side? Whose odor and bodyshape does he carry upon him, under his clothes? Who began the day with her, waking from sleep together in the same bed; together with whom did he or she wake?"

Sometimes, when all the world below seemed aqueous, the night lights shining in the watery glass panes of buildings, he thought of himself as anchored like a buoy out in the waters, and a warning and a limit. Or it seemed as though he were on a boat riding upon an ocean of trees and rooftops, heads and hats, where the streets of the city were waterpaths, ocean roads and channels, and where distant mountains rose and fell into desert and prairie and level land like humps and spreadings-out of waves; the breathing of ocean, the lights upon it, as of many ships and boats, the steeple across from him where the cross mocked him, and the pole of the weathervane where the turning cock mocked him, the church across the street whose great window was like a stone wheel with silver spokes of metal dividing countries that told of the story of Adam and Eve and of their sons and of the lands they went out into, returning, round the story of the wheel, to Adam and Eve, again, round and round, the round story of precious glasses that shone and glimmered in the day and night light. He was in the air, then, companion to weathercock and steeplecross and flag, bird and weather.

Sometimes he saw a person walking as though sinking in the flood of humanity like a drowning man, and he wished he could throw down the lifeline of the fire rope by his window and tied to his bed, or a raft of the mattress of his single bed, or some lifebuoy to save him; and to those adrift in the current and rushing stream of the sidewalk hurtling toward what cataract or chasm at what street crossing or corner, he would have cried down beware! or here take this helping hand of rescue!—and would those below who might be drowning or adrift have mocked him, who were the betrayers of the man on the flagpole? He looked down at the burnt-looking sides of buildings where the spidery fire escapes clung like webs; saw the acorn-shaped watertowers on their shafts; saw the blind man on the corner (crying "I'm looking out for you!") with his red and white striped crutch; saw mutterers shuffling along; saw some wiping tears, saw waiters, people lingering for somebody who, when he arrived, would be no help at all; saw meetings; saw dumbshows of conversations, saw what could be murders, thefts, crimes . . . saw all the humanity.

Once, for all day and most of all night, he watched through his binoculars in a faraway swimming ark of a building, a lonely person in his room, sitting on the side of his bed as though his mind were gathering to it all things it loved and remembered to store and keep there in one room. In time he saw the lonely person rise from his bed and take to his own eyes a pair of binoculars and come to the window to look straight across the waves of lower buildings at him as if he had known all along that he was there; and for a moment of terror their eyes were against each other so close that it seemed their lashes might brush. It was, at that moment, as though they were two solitudes meeting each other without telling of it, and joining each other, as though they called across great distances and over all the traffic of humanity to each other, *hello! hello!* and heard each other's answer. And then Chris knew that he was here, removed and yet at home again, because he had made some choice, with the help of Marvello, and to keep it; that he had anchored his heart, his Self in the depths or lofts of his beginnings and he watched the world of it from his perch as though he were on a buoy. He knew, now, what had raised him up there, and he knew what could bring him down: the idea of himself.

The city and the life of it below might have been his temptation, for all things he desired were there among the living members of the world; yet he was no longer involved—and still he *was* involved.

Why was it that every time he went into this human traffic, involved in it, he was wounded or murdered? He must understand or continue to suffer damage and error and to inflict these. To find someone in whom and through whom he could love the life of the human world, and through whom he could put it to some order! Otherwise it was chaos and murder and maiming of self. This is the only search, he knew . . . love . . . all else begins there at that beginning: this is the turning back that takes one ahead; and within each of us lies this little Beginningness. So that was why he was here, to protect the *idea* which it seemed the world tried to maim, and to revive and to wait for the little Beginningness that would surely happen if one loved it enough to nurse it back into health and wholeness.

Someone! he thought. Someone through whom he could perceive the world, love the world and his own race, through whom and to whom he could relate what had happened to him in the broad world, through whom he could order all that had happened to him and, being *together, begin* together, and so understand all their errors and crimes, all single woe. This was the only way, the spiritual way, this man of sensuality thought, of fulfilling, realizing, using one's human life. The way of the *idea,* this man of nature thought, is the way to possess the world through another human being, as human beings hold the world within themselves, within their divine gift of carrying in themselves the idea; the search is for that, he knew, now. Each man carries crime and murder and salvation and re-creation of the world within himself, and he carries within him the laws of nature which enlighten him of these. We can reach these no other way than through each other, through loving each other. The destiny of the world and of the race is in a human body, in the flesh and in the spirit of the human body. To walk through the fields and the limitless territory of the beloved body, to live in the landscape of the beloved face, to inhabit the round universe of the mind of the beloved . . . all the world, all history, past and present and future, all myths and legends and tales of conflict and pacification, sin and expiation, exist within this body crowned by the living idea which inhabits it and will not be brought down . . . or if it falls, we fall; until some rescuer raises it again, aloft; honor it, praise it, love it, protect it. It is when we find this readiness in another that we rise up, whole and live and in each other and in love. This, he thought, is the hope of men: to make the choice of love and keep it; to search, waiting in the possession of this choice. Without this choice, this loss, we live in a kind of battle with life and with other human beings and with ourselves, a daily panic. The "successes" of human life only lead us away from the choice and away from ourselves to betray both, and away from our *living place*, which is within ourselves, and away from love and the beloved we seek who is waiting in the possession of his own soul for someone else who has made the choice and kept it. So every day we are destroying and committing crimes against the very one who waits and whom we seek. The only evil lies in those who never made the choice, or never kept it, who want to destroy the chooser and the beginner, to maim him and wreck his beginningness and so keep him from rebuilding, recreating the world in that image. Someone, he thought, in a great burst of joy and hope, to lead us back to where we began and who stands there, waiting to take us up, and so to start again to rebuild the world in the image of that beginning!

For the first time he saw all this so clearly as to be ready to put it down as the truth he had sought, and this in the territory of persecution and of the blind, mindless, faithless who had abused and ridiculed and tormented his own beloved and secret image, his own countrymen. He felt himself, at last, the lover brother full of a radiant and merciful forgiveness until, when the double-edged pendulum of his searching casuistry, having swung to its farthest on that side, cut back in the opposite direction, slashing through his hope and restoring the terrible precarious balance: he saw, too—and this was the greatest revelation and one which he knew, now, he could only see at *home,* where it all lived and had begun—that he, like all the others, had taken to himself the image to use for his own secret meaning. I am guilty as all the others, he thought; I have justified my own claim and set myself against the claims of the others; I, alas, am like all the others, guilty where they are guilty, innocent where they are innocent: we *are* together, my family, my race! We must help one another! But he saw, then, how he had pursued his own secret idea of the Flagpole Sitter, had followed it over all the world and had tracked it down to its source again where he would face it to whatever conclusion he could bring it to. *Here was the difference!* he thought, as he walked up and down the room, justifying himself again. But *was* there a difference between him and those below who, though they had stayed in the territory of the idea, might have traveled unmeasured and unrecorded journeys of distress and anguish in the same search as his? Was the whole long bitter traveling for nothing; had nobody come anywhere?

He had heard, from time to time, what he thought was a knock on his door; but he thought it either a remoter noise and not a hand on his door, or the figment of his own secret wish that someone would come up the stairs to his door. At any rate, and whatever it was, he had ignored the knocking sound.

He began to suffer the goading urge to go down the stairs and onto the street, and took, now, to cracking the door to peep down. Often he thought he saw faces on the stairs. He was a fugitive! a prisoner in the galleries of his own mind where image after image of himself followed each other, leading him further and further into himself. Who would deliver him? One morning when he opened the door to look down the steps, he found to his surprise a basket covered with cloth. When he brought in the basket and opened it, he found a variety of foods, milk, coffee and delicacies, but no note to say who had brought these to him, only a message written neatly on a sheet of folded paper which said, "I have seen your face and recognized you, Marvello!" Pasted below the words was a photograph of Ishbel's son Pietro! That long-vanished face, as though it were out of a tale Chris had been told, now seemed so unbelievable. Though it looked worn by suffering and anonymity, this face still had that half-look which that member, so young then, of his once splendid family that had led him away and was destroyed by him, could not name. He ate a few bits from the basket and pinned the photograph of the lovely brother Pietro on the wall by the window. Now the photograph was a link between all that happened in his unaccountable past and the stark surety of his present.

His nights were becoming unbearably lonely, now. As the city slept, he hovered over it and watched it. He was coming to terms with it, some reconciliation was at hand, but it was coming through slow agony. How many more were at their windows of lonely dark rooms, watching the world below? And what were their reasons? How many sensed him up there? How many dreams of sleepers in all the houses and buildings did he disturb? He watched with his binoculars now with longing and hottest desire what had begun dispassionately and what he thought was with carelessness. In his fantasia of loneliness he saw naked young men and women at their curtained windows looking up at him, caressing their own bodies as they made whispering shapes with their lips, calling out to one they longed for; and he saw them walk up and down, tormented, in their vacant rooms; saw lovers loving—and how he desired the world below him, now! For he had seen, it seemed, everything the world did, in secret. He had watched the whole show and participated in it; he had seen families in rooms making decisions, and partings of members of families. He was tormented by the behavior of the world, in what he had thought would be his sanctuary from the world. If someone would appear! One time a face suddenly rose up at his window and gazed at him, and though he wanted to cry to it at once, *come in!,* he snatched down the blind in such ferocity that it collapsed to the floor as he saw the legs and feet of a human figure rising up beyond the windowpane and vanish, as though it were an ascension; but it was a window-cleaner hoisting himself up.

Was he taking too much upon himself, too much human life for human life to bear? Would he go mad at his window and, in the end, throw himself down upon the world below, destroying himself upon the very body of the world he was removed from? Would he, in the end, be the victim of this life below, though it would never know it, moving along its way ignorant of what hung and suffered above it, and never even knowing that it had destroyed him? He went on watching—the quarrels of lovers in rooms; men counting money on tables that was earned or stolen or saved. All he watched, now, seemed to be trying to discover someone with whom to find and make a peaceable way of life and to keep it, together: this struggle of love, as simple as that, this fierce battle, through the loins and the heart, as though people fought each other with these instruments of warfare; cannon did not then seem to him, in his watching, more powerful. He longed to be involved in this beautiful and terrible, damned strife; he longed to be destroyed by it.

But would he turn on what deviled him, again, and seek, again, this time fully aware and with the responsibility of his act fallen upon himself and no other, the destruction? Would he, then, become *his own scapegoat, his own victim, his own death,* committing upon the others what they had, in his past, committed upon him, make *them* his scapegoat as they had made him theirs, this time deliberately? His little space around the window became the livingplace of Cain, where violence and suspicion followed by selfdevouring and self-questioning approached him to the edge of madness. Who would come up the stairs to him to find him gone, *destroyed by himself in the act of trying to recover himself,* vanished, as though eaten up, devoured by himself in an attempt to possess himself, with only the savage remains of his voracious life to show of him? What deliverer of him, what savior, dreaming of him, would come up to him at the last minute to rescue him, to tell him that he could only see himself if he had been *two people,* but come too late, to find him torn to pieces by his own hand as if he had been no more than a composition of letters and photographs . . . who had come, having it on his tongue to say to him as he opened the door to his knock, "Marvello Marvello I have found you at last. I have come to join you and follow you, and together and with Cain as our invisible brother we will make a beginning and a new world built on the truth of ourselves, who know through our suffering and our deaths and our love that we are everyman, and not exceptions to them. Our beginning will be based on the murderer and the lover in us all, it will not deny or betray its ancestry and its brotherhood. It will not will away its dark brotherhood, it will go halt, crippled by its own race, and it will mend itself and with the help of its own race; it will pardon and show mercy; and it will be built on human love, which is a strife and a clashing. It will not commit the murderous act of assassinating the flesh any more than it will mutilate the idea and the spirit. It will be a race of rescuers and savers, of protectors and defenders against *the killer-self forever coming upon the quiet creator-self in us,* the laborer of half-love and half-hate where he works in his fields." And Chris caught himself crying out, into his empty window-space, "When will he come, when will Marvello come to Marvello, the lover brother to the killer brother?" and sobbing so loudly as he cried out that if passersby on the sidewalk below could have heard him they should have thought him a madman and sent for the police. In his most extreme agony, he went to his door, opened it and heard his own foot upon the stair. It was midnight. He had come, at last, to his own rescue.

He wandered in the cold. He did not look for one instant at those he had so longed for, aloft, who seemed so desirable from his window. It was the distance that had made the difference. He knew, like an animal, where he was going. It was to the building where he had seen the other man with the binoculars.

When he came to the building, a shabby tenement house, it was completely dark and he knew he could not follow his plan until daylight. He went to the park nearby and slept there until mid-morning, for he would never again return to that room he had escaped. He woke in the world and rose and went straight to the tenement house. He asked the Landlady if there was an available room on the fifth floor to be let by the week; and she showed him to a dirty room with a bed and a table, a dresser and a calendar, and he took it. As he had known and planned, without advising himself of it, it was next door to the other man's, whom he knew to be Pietro.

For the first time he was free, for he had wrought his identity clean and clear, and out of the world of that city where he had been anonymous and unnamed so long ago, named and proclaimed in so many others but, he knew now, dishonestly, though ever so slightly dishonestly, veiled by the image that he was rapidly tearing from his face and his body, like film or gauze, to bring his final nakedness. After an hour in his room, listening and looking out through the binoculars upon himself in his other window across the buildings, eye to eye, he heard the rustlings of his neighbor, Pietro. Pietro was having a conversation with himself. He was planning Chris's death. He was going to shoot Chris. His earlier plan, he declared to himself, of hiding a poisonous snake in the basket of food at Chris's door had been decided against. Pietro was going to kill him by gunfire and he would do it tonight, Chris heard him declaring to himself.

Chris waited all afternoon, and the night of his murder was approaching. Should he sit there, separated only by a wall from his murderer and wait for him to fire his gun at him and then, as he sat by his window, his gun smoking and at rest and peace in his trembling hand, open his door and cry "Pietro!" and watch him turn to him with the look of death and bewilderment in his face as he saw the same look in his victim's?

Suddenly, after unbearable spaces of utter quiet, Chris could hear Pietro moan and tumble on his bed. Then, as though Pietro were exhausted, and Chris, too, Pietro fell dead quiet and Chris could hear him breathing heavily in the troubled sleep he had fallen into.

Should he go into Pietro's room and have a conversation with him that might bring their long enmity to other persuasions? Should he save himself, or Pietro? But there was no question of "salvation." There could be no "loss," either, for it would come back, in the mind and the memory, in the conscience, all the whole search and flight and haunted stalking, the last paralysis: the halting in one room before one window, staring at the opposite image as though it were a still fish in a stagnant bowl.

It was darkening now and no light in Chris's room, only the glancing and shifting light of electric signs in the street below. Chris took his binoculars and went to the window to look once more and for the last time at the other window across the city. For a moment it was as though he were Shipwreck Kelley huddled there. And then he saw such a look on his face that he was glad that it was going to be forever obliterated by the gunfire of Pietro. He surrendered it. Then he went back to his bed against the dividing wall from Pietro's bed and placed the pillows against the wall, stretched himself out on his back with his ear to the wall, and waited. Pietro was against the wall, too, on his bed, and breathing heavily. For the last time Chris said to himself, "No, I will not have a conversation with him, my murderer, though only a thin wall separates us upon our beds." That was final. He took a deep breath.

But he began to feature how it would be, the murder: It would be time. He would hear Pietro go to his window and arrange himself there, then the click of his trigger as he cocked it. Pietro would wait, who had seen Chris so often and nothing else but him through the lenses of his binoculars that he no longer knew when he did not see him—Chris lived in the lenses as though he inhabited the binoculars; his face was stamped forever upon the lenses of Pietro's eyes. Then Pietro would fire.

In a moment, before those who heard the gunfire could get there to see what happened, Chris would hear Pietro on the stairs and then closing the street door behind him. At his window, Chris would see Pietro running down the street in the flashing lights of signs, the fugitive. He knew where Pietro would go, up Chris's own stairs, through Chris's own door and to his window to claim Chris's body there.

And Pietro would know that Chris was waiting for him there in what he would find, the remains of decaying food, the destroyed letters, the obscured photograph. They would only have exchanged windows.

Then Chris would leave his room and go into Pietro's, to Pietro's window, and there find the debris of what Pietro had left, like his own. He would sit down in Pietro's chair by the window, take Pietro's binoculars and look through them to see, through the other window, Pietro astonished and crazed at finding no body of Chris where he had thought to have destroyed it, his lips forming over and over again the shape of the called name, "Marvello! Marvello!"

And just as Chris would see Pietro take up his binoculars and look over at his own window to find in the lenses Chris's face, Chris would hear the people coming in the door to capture him, the murderer; and when he felt the hands of those who were his old neighbors and townspeople and, perhaps, even some of his own kin, but, above all, his captors, upon his shoulders and heard their question, "What happened?", he knew that he could never tell them what had gone on so long and what was ended, only murmur, clutching himself, "I have been wounded; but the other man is dead."

No. It must take another turn. He was at the crossing—and he would go on, over, this time, and end the whole long preparation. To begin! To reconcile his dangerous brother! To marry darkness and light, murder and life, love and hate that had pursued and haunted and crippled each other all over the world and now were back where they had started, crouching in small animal spaces with only a wall separating them. Destroy the wall! he cried out to himself, with the courage and love to find and follow one's own nature, to find a spiritual basis for a life of sensual action, to find and follow one's own human nature, and to understand it, the light and the darkness of it, struggling for the possession of one's self and the freedom to use one's discovered self, turning it more and more to the center of light that lies, even, in the darkness. To rescue my own nature, in the face of killers of nature, of dictators, of standards and styles and patterns; and not to die through this courage but come to more life by it. Not to compensate for childhood but to season the childhood image and walk away with it through manhood, erect and proud and fierce. To oppose and to combat the Compensators, the cult of freaks, of the monstrous, of the bizarre, the passionate sickness, the frail deformed, the undersize, the outsize, the exquisite diseased, the ego-ridden, the victimizers, the avengers. To oppose these by simplicity and by daring, by romantic love, by a classic cleanliness, by heroic friendship or by a personal, lonely heroism . . . by an *abidingness*. I am at the crossing.

Now it was time. He heard Pietro going to his window and he heard him arrange himself there. Then he heard the click of his trigger.

Softly, from his bed against the wall he whispered, "Pietro! Pietro!"; and he heard Pietro start, then wait cunningly like an animal in the bush. "Pietro! Pietro!" he whispered through the wall.

He heard Pietro leap from his chair at the window and rush to his door. He knew Pietro's ear was against the door. "Pietro! Pietro!" he called, louder this time; and then Pietro, who knew the calling of his name was from the direction of the wall, rushed to his bed and leaped upon it, and Chris heard his ear searching against the wall, passionately, trying to detect the source of the call.

Chris tapped on the wall, waited a moment, then put his mouth there and whispered . . . "Why do you persecute me who am your salvation?" And then Chris heard Pietro call, breathing as if he were dying . . . "Marvello!"

Pietro lay back on his bed and Chris on his, and they talked through the wall, their mouths pressed against it. They joined, first with that distance between them, then closer and closer until they were pressed against the wall that divided them so closely that they could feel, it seemed, the warmth and shape of each other's bodies; and finally, the door to Chris's room opened and Pietro, his half-brother, stood there, with half a look of dangerousness and half a look of love. And then he came slowly to Chris and they joined utterly.

The next morning, early, they left the city, the one of them. And where they went was over the ways of perilous brotherhood and love.

What crimes and violence produced out of this fierce tension of

damned and blessed brotherhood, what magnificent works of serene and breathless beauty, seeming, to the world, to have been
showered up as effortlessly and as carelessly as the spray by the wing-
touch of one dragonfly skiffing upon a pool, would we hear about
in the time ahead, but forged by the gigantic thrashing and turning
of this grinding stone wheel of warfare and peace within a single
being? To measure the shape made is the only permanent story to
be told; and to struggle to name it: two halves warring and pacifying
us along, time after time, age after age.

The Nurse's Epilogue

Now it is well nigh dawning and, as I told you at the beginning, this
tale is finished with the light of day. The rest belongs to darkness,
whence it came. I hope I have seized it out of darkness and brought
it, this tale, into the light for a little while. I have told you this story
as I best could, and if I have imputed to this life you have heard
about from my mouth anything spurious or alien to it, if I have em-
bellished it or adorned it or misshaped it in the manner old storytellers have of garnishing and enlarging upon the tale they have
to tell—so much comes into a story that seems to belong to it in the
telling, and as you go along, that you had never seen to belong
there when you started—it is because there is that mysterious attraction, that unaccountable contribution all things seem to suffer
with and yield up to the inventor, as though all the living and buried
world were alerted to the telling of one story. Stories have their own
life and growth and you must let them take to themselves all they
need to nourish and strengthen themselves—*I* believe. You must,
if you can see to it, indulge me and take it as a well-meant fiction;
and understand that a Nurse must have some fiction in his life that
is often such a solitary sitting, as though he were a single keeper of
an isolated pumping station or a power plant beyond great living
places. That source and fountainhead of power, providing for so
many far away and using its provision so matter-of-factly, fuel or
light or water, can come to mean whatever the keeper and tender of
it has a mind or reverie to make of it in his lonely imagination in
order to keep a sense of stronger duty to it, if for no other reason.
And he is bound to lend to it a great portion of himself and his own
dreaming mind—some shape of life that is, like human life itself,
both real (and of the commonest creature use), and fantastic. For

often, and in those extraordinarily active secret reveries of removed fertile fancies, the materials of human daily life are mean and impoverished, daily incidents and tasks do not take or use all they have to give, and some energy or some yearning is uninvolved and left over to work on simple subjects and objects before them—on their supper table or in their small room, whatever is available in the landscape where they are, what grows or grazes or was built there, in the country where they live—to take on more life than their daily life provides. This country, this invented or remade country is the country where they *live*, no other place. Men have used windmills, figures made of clay or paint, the moon, mountains, boats built in their backyards that never touched an ocean, to this end and out of this human energy of which I speak; and I have made use of this infirm human body, spread out before me, turning on and on, this engine, the voice beneath it, in its own process of healing, this incalculable and mysterious and magnificently complicated, infinitely devious and ever-changing human body that is a universe no man can ever fully know or ably describe but continues, over and over again, to try his hand at if he loves it. Begin with love.

Old nurses, superannuated and the healing out of their hands, nurse over again all that was sick and wounded and needed help towards healing and see, later, so much more of the healing process and what was healed, than then. All the world heals in one healing injured man: regenerate him and you regenerate the world. I think it is the worthiest task in this human world; and I would do it all again, had I to do it or were I called to it.

I go a step farther, though, before I end this Record, and say that I think I had in my charge and under my meditation and consideration the very representative and symbol of that age and day and time, and that my patient was the very healing consciousness of that time, that time of the crippled mind, that time of the world when human beings, not being able to tell the truth about themselves, could not tell it about other people and so maimed themselves and everything they touched: that time of the crutch-war of the cripples; that time when the nervous hunting mind, that burned country of the brain, found only the surface glister and the small melodramatic woe surrounding the failure of a pickup in a bar or the insult suffered round a tea table, and the deep undermind, the dreaming mind that finds the permanent, lay paralyzed. What would bring these two together again, except the wrestling of one human being with his human race to achieve again what, it seemed to him, his race had deprived him of or what he had robbed of his society?—his other heroic self, a past glory; to lift the veil, the mask from the image and see it fully and honestly in the face . . . and marry it or murder it. And who is the opponent in this wrestling match but the boring sage who simplifies, the triumphant perpetuator of the half-truth who reproduces life as it is dishonestly and blindly lived. The cure, the healing? Only that we try to exceed ourselves, that we strive towards that, that we work to enlighten ourselves and that we be just and merciful in that work. *This* is the story to be told. Something is wounded and heals within each of us, within his solitary secret little tent; love and compassion tend the wound and lend hand to the healing; but we are curing ourselves . . . this is the process of life and the destiny of the world working through each single human being, and what obstructs that, what works against it, impedes it, delays it or destroys it, is evil, is murder. This machine of healing, this process, toils and spins from its own inner source. If its energy comes from anywhere outside its own core or center, it is false, it does not heal, it does not make marrow.

But before I seem to you to be too cocksure, too self-justifying, let me air you my tormenting doubt. Was I at the loom when I should have been at the window? When I worked the loom, what went unworked at through the window? Did loom rob me of window, window rob me of loom? My impossible task was to fuse loom and window, one expressing the other and brought to order through me, the manipulator and the watcher: my work that led me almost to madness was to reach that point when what was on the loom and what was beyond the window became one.

And did I create a being or *an idea of a being* that will haunt and follow me all my life? Did I salvage up out of my depths of my patient a sunken image which was *mine*, not his? For I tell you I saw this shape before me, and having only some facts, some details, fantasticated the rest—old fantastic healer, fabulous artificer that I am, curse or blessing be it. And did I give it to him to go away with . . . a disordered and dangerous idea shaped and clarified to positive use in the world of men? Or is he searching for me, his thief and murderer, to blame me for what I borrowed from him and lent to him, to gain his vengeance upon me—and to reclaim his Notebook? Does he love me for what I showed and gave him, and hate me, too, with Cain's hate? Sometimes I fear that the image I have made, put together with such pain and self-expense—most of my years have gone, now, into the meditation of it—and let loose in the wide world, will turn on *me,* in the end, and destroy what created it, what has taken on the image, itself, what has *become* the invention and has had to go through the whole life of it again, this time for *myself,* my life has been so disturbed by it.

But begin with the love that re-makes. And there you have the ending of this Record, and its whole meaning, in the Beginning.

—CURRAN
At the Lighthouse

VII

When I closed this strange, disturbing and veiled record, I found myself, as the new Lighthouse Keeper, compelled to carry on a little farther its thought put into me, and for *myself*. I thought, as I copied it down to keep for myself and to show to others when I might—for I would surrender Curran's Log to the Captain when he came for it—how, if someone were to put a long time and great patience—and love for what this old man had struggled to tell—into it, he might come down from the Lighthouse one day with a marvelous thing to tell. But that someone would have to try to bring the story to finish.

To bring to finish! Is anything human ever brought to end? As soon as it reaches its fullest expression it shatters like a wild rose into all the pieces that miraculously clove together to compose it: this may be the only steady progress in the human world: and on and on it goes: can we ever hold the perfect unshattering blossom in our hand?

As the last sentence is put down, as though it were of stretched rubber, pulling the whole pattern to its fastening of a period, the final period is only the little knot that, touched and broken loose by a wandering, searching finger, snaps back through the whole taut weaving and thrusts it back again into a knotted chaos—for someone else, who follows, to shape again. Is there any permanent shape? any . . . "progress"? But I must stop this question, for I shall be beginning the whole thing over again. Here is the final little knot   .   I leave it to you, to touch or leave fast.

But is there any rest from it?

Now dawn is breaking, and the Wake is over, and I settle down to begin my own long work in Curran's image. But look—is that a small boat rowing towards me, with one figure sitting in it? And is it coming for me?

—MARVELLO
At the Lighthouse

Afterword

REGINALD GIBBONS

In addition to the many stories this book tells, there are two stories about it. One is the story of what kind of a book it is, and the other is the story of the writing of the book and its not having been published before now. The first story is about the writer's art, his desires, his vision. The other is about his having been thwarted by circumstances and lack of understanding, and brought to doubt his own artistic vision and his accomplishment.

William Goyen was in no way a realist, in either his aesthetic or the practical sense. As a writer, he felt no interest in the illusion of a realistic fictional theater in the mind, within which characters spoke and acted in plausible settings. Rather, he created images and fables to convey the reality of feeling. Perhaps one of the artistic lessons Goyen offers us is the power and memorableness of his inventive play of narrators and form, but it's a play not for ingenuity's sake, and not in order to signal the reader that the fiction-writer is quite conscious of his methods and devices (as other experimenters with the novel have done). Goyen's play and experimentation with the novel are for the sake of extending the emotional reach of fiction deeper and deeper into our being. He took from D. H. Lawrence, among other artistic models, a passionate fidelity to the storms and calms of feeling hidden within us rather than to the outward appearances, habits, and obligations that we live by. Goyen rejected the material of "realistic" fiction quite as definitively as any poet might have done, refusing to write such sentences as—in the French poet Paul Valéry's famous quip—"The Marquise went out at five o'clock." Goyen persisted in writing what he felt to be true to his sense of life, rather than a response to the perceived market for fiction. His own definition of "style"—a "transformation of the material"—exemplifies his desire to create a way of writing that had little to do with realism.

Rather, the sense of life in Goyen's fiction is centered on the transforming power of love and spirit and the transporting (and sometimes deranging) power of the erotic. Goyen represents the erotic as having two faces—sheer energy and ecstasy, and also a torment of feeling. From the very beginning, in fact, Goyen found words and form for bafflement, unknowing, and frustrated desire, as well as for rapture. He wrote about our being in conflict with ourselves, experiencing both joy and fear, appetite and revulsion, tenderness and violence, as these feelings and impulses war against each other to dominate the erotic moment and identity itself: "with half a look of hate and half a look of love."

In his first two books, the novel *The House of Breath* (1950) and the collection of short stories *Ghost and Flesh* (1952), Goyen portrayed sexual experience, whether heterosexual or homosexual, as a journey (not necessarily physical) to self-discovery, self-creation, identity. The erotic could be a reclaiming of the life of the spirit, deeper than the life of appearances or the material life of the everyday world; but erotic desire could also become ungovernable, could inflict wounds. In Goyen's fiction, the erotic is a demon or angel within us that not only occupy our body but also cries down the corridors of our spirit. It transcends gender and sexual preference.

While the fables in *Half a Look of Cain*[1] are not only about sexuality—both straight and gay, both physical and symbolic—desire lies at the heart of each. Goyen's fable of the nurse says that all physical touch is erotic; his tale of Chris and Stella says that physical love is a world unto itself; his tale of Pietro and Marvello says that erotic love can torment a relationship of brotherhood, or, contrarily, create brotherhood out of desire. Marvello's career and the bizarre acts of the flagpole sitter say that the erotic can tinge the experience of being celebrated by audiences, of being seen and attended to; the fable of the hospital in the flood says that the realm of healing and human touch is an animal paradise which, like that of the ark, makes companions of former enemies; and the very structure of the novel, like that of nearly all Goyen's fiction, says that the unfolding of a story can be a kind of erotic interplay between teller and listener.

The inimitably Goyenesque chain of linked ideas in *Half a Look of Cain* is something like this: We are all damaged in life by those occasions when we are spurned, turned away, forgotten, left behind, excluded; and then we too may hurt and exclude. We may be healed, although we cannot heal until we acknowledge the damage and the damaging impulse inside us; love and desire can be a path toward that acknowledgment and that healing. Healed, or even still healing, we can see that life is both terribly painful and an incomprehensible marvel (such as a circus performer, Marvello, can approach embodying), full of unaccountable dangers and joys. And we want to tell of such experiences, and to hear of them, for the telling and listening in themselves heal us and give us to each other.

Raptures and desolations of feeling, including struggles against one's own self, were what Goyen particularly wanted to find a way to portray in his fiction, believing as he did that they were so much of life, yet mostly absent from the new fiction of his time. "And where they went was over the ways of perilous brotherhood and love," *Half a Look of Cain* says of two characters, their "crimes and violence" as well as their "magnificent works of serene and breathless beauty . . . forged by the gigantic thrashing and turning of this grinding stone wheel of warfare and peace within a single being." As we strive to achieve what we desire and to understand what we do, Goyen suggests, there are "two halves warring and pacifying us along, time after time, age after age."

In fact, Goyen's focus on conflict, self-contradiction, opposed brothers, men loving and hating each other, man with and against woman, is transformed into a fictional method in his lifelong insistence that fiction is always a small drama of telling, is always the confrontation of two beings, one who tells and one who listens. This pairing and opposition, this simultaneity of two opposed roles, informs his artistic decisions about structure, voice and language. The many pairs of characters in *Half a Look of Cain* are a thematic expression of this same idea—the Biblical Cain and his brother appear and reappear in Marvello and Pietro, in Chris and the distant flagpole sitter who is the true father of his child with Stella, in Curran the nurse and Chris his patient, in Chris and Pietro, and even, as that last section of the novel implies, within one and the same Chris. A desperate need for love and a tormented impulse to flee or destroy love produce a constant exploratory movement of both feeling and form in the novel.

Half a Look of Cain is also a hidden link in Goyen's experiments with novelistic structure: he constructed *The House of Breath* as a group of "medallions" spoken in different voices (although there is something like a central point of view in the mind of the narrator, who breathes the voices of others to life, and then is breathed by them into deeper life of his own). Goyen shaped *Half a Look of Cain* by nesting stories within stories, again changing narrative voices but this time creating a structure of concentric circles of narration—a method that almost makes the novel seem to turn or swirl slowly in a circle, a marvelously compact yet majestic structure; the book is brief but filled with a surprising number of characters and tales, all of them in relation to each other like planets in orbit around the same sun of feeling. Goyen's nesting of tales within tales, narrators within narrations, complicates the reader's usual expectations and experience of sequentiality, and also sidesteps our expectation that a narrator will be always and foremost himself and just himself. The narrator of the outer-circle episodes of *Half a Look of Cain* tells us the contents of an autobiographical Record that he has found in the isolated lighthouse of which he is the new keeper. This Record reveals his predecessor to have been a male nurse during World War II and afterward. The nurse describes one patient in particular, and then gives us, in turn, the contents of that patient's notebook. There is even one tale that is the nurse's writing of a story on behalf of the patient, as if from inside the patient's knowledge and experience, not his own. We are certainly a long way from the predictable contours of the first-person novel which cannot lift itself out of the limits of its narrator's, and often its author's, own experience. Goyen's imagination is, by comparison, prodigious, and *Half a Look of Cain,* even more than *The House of Breath,* is one of the most subtly, richly constructed American experiments in the novel. The implications and interrelations of its many interruptions, voices, images, echoes and reiterations, are astonishingly complex. The novel is a kind of tapestry with repeated figures, each repetition a new variation of the pattern.

Why the redundancy of sheer telling in *Half a Look of Cain* and other fiction by Goyen? He believed that *story* is not only an entertainment, a meaningful reshaping of the often senseless acts and events of life as it is actually lived, but also a constitutive experience that creates our humanity and establishes the bonds between us. One person listens, another tells. So lovers and friends and cousins and brothers and married couples, uncles with their nephews (to list some of the pairs of tellers and listeners in Goyen's fiction), are not only human beings bound to each other but also a part of the creation of identity; they are hidden dramas taking place as one person is hearing the other tell some secret or revelation or answer, or some haunting question, that in itself partly defines both teller and listener as persons. And beyond all this, these pairs of tellers and listeners are also models of a spiritual journey from ignorance to understanding, from lovelessness to love, from solitude and loneliness to a web of sustaining relationships, from alienation to affiliation.

Of course, we don't read *Half a Look of Cain* just to find out what else Goyen discovered he could do with the form of the novel. We read to be transported, "moved," our imaginations engaged and our sense of life extended. *Half a Look of Cain* rewards us in both ways. When we read it we are drawn into the novel as a project of human inventiveness and feeling and art; we are drawn deeper into an abundance of emotional life and artistic play. This was how, implicitly, Goyen defined human life: story, struggle, insight. Anguish and elation.

The other story of *Half a Look of Cain* is of the writing of it and its not having been published till now.

Goyen began to write sketches that would eventually become part of *The House of Breath* during the Second World War, when he was serving in the navy. From a hospital in Oregon, where he was treated for the migraines that had effectively disqualified him from further sea duty, he returned to Texas. Decommissioned, he felt restless and confined in his parents' house. The problem of home and away was gnawing at him. He later told of bringing his mother home from the hospital after an illness, and of her saying to him, as soon as she entered the house and saw Goyen's suitcase packed and standing near the door, "If you leave, I'll die." And of his saying to her in reply, "If I don't leave, I'll die."

With a navy friend, Walter Berns, he went west. In the decade when he wrote *The House of Breath, Ghost and Flesh,* and *Half a Look of Cain,* Goyen lived off and on near Taos, New Mexico. Then he moved from this physical seclusion to the East, for some years living in and around Manhattan. To some extent, this decisive move answered a desire to end his isolation, to be near other writers and publishing. And yet in some way Goyen, like the great Modernists who were his literary beacons—Pound and Eliot, he said, especially—remained a provincial, with the provincial's peculiar disadvantage and advantage once he reaches the metropolitan world that was already there, glittering and imposing, before he arrived. However seduced he is by it, he brings with him a more intense impression of art precisely because he has come from where art was mostly absent. Nor is the provincial usually able to betray the formative world he had left behind, its voices. And these voices, so unselfconscious, are the root stock of the provincial's triumphant art, when he attains such, in the terms of the great city.

For the provincial feels a great loss and a great gain at the same time, a tormenting contradiction. The voices of the past, of the home place, can never be heard again in unself-conscious authenticity, nor can the provincial ever speak that language again without a double consciousness. If *Half a Look of Cain* is above all a fictional meditation on desire, it is also, in its images of longing and love, of loneliness and companionship, a meditation on the social portion of identity, beyond a psychological and sexual part. Goyen's work is filled with fictional meditation on the troubled, even tormented, alienation of the individual from his origins—persons are always leaving home and returning in his fiction, unable to bear being at home among those who do not understand them and unable to bear being away. Thus Chris/Shipwreck Kelley, Chris/Marvello, in the last and most fantastic episode of the novel, is struck by a revelation of his oneness with his origins, but cannot hold onto it, and is still caught between joy at feeling akin to his own people and dismay and even despair at feeling so different from them—akin in his participation in the dailiness of life, his relatedness to them all, his need for love, his being a member of the group of them; and yet different in the secret individuality of his being, in his ambitions, his desires.

The publication of *The House of Breath* made Goyen, for a moment, a literary celebrity in both New York and Texas, and won him grants. Goyen later told of how after the publication of *The House of Breath* he felt for a while that everyone he met in the literary world wanted a piece of him, wanted to admire him as the moment's fashion, and yet at the same time he felt that others were angry at him for his moment of public recognition. Goyen was said by some of his acquaintances of those years to have himself felt great envy of the public recognition of other writers. Something in this private experience of the writer is transformed in *Half a Look of Cain* into the figure of Marvello, who not only is admired and hated for his accomplishment, but also cannot help feeling that his success has estranged him from others, and even begins to feel the impulse to destroy what he has made.

In any event, the critical success of *The House of Breath* did not secure Goyen's position with his publisher; nor could it resolve the life problem of being home or away. Goyen's mother, and perhaps the rest of his family, had already strenuously disapproved of his fiction; and the book did not sell. Some such defeat was to meet Goyen with the publication of every book. However, who would choose to characterize such a writer as a failure at making a living at fiction? To define his career in the only terms that have any lasting meaning would be to say, instead, that despite the disappointments of his career as a writer, Goyen was able to create and sustain a unique style and fictional vision that enriched American letters, expanded the possibilities of the novel, and unforgettably touched the lives of many readers. The next step in this artistic project, despite the hope of his publishers that he would write something popular, was to be *Half a Look of Cain*.

The germ of experience that appears to have provided Goyen with the central donnée of *Half a Look of Cain* can be found in his letter of January 5, 1950, to Spud Johnson:

> I fell down about sixty magnificent marble stairs de-
> signed by Michelangelo in Rome—the famous "Spanish
> steps" and badly injured my right knee. I tore loose the
> cartilage and now nothing but an operation will mend
> it—I can scarcely walk and then only by going stiff-
> legged.[2]

Ten days later, in a letter to James Laughlin, the director of New Directions, with whom he was corresponding about a translation that he hoped would be published, Goyen wrote:

> Two days ago the doctors told me I must have an opera-
> tion at once; something is torn loose inside the joint.
> This means three weeks in hospital and three weeks re-
> conditioning of the leg.

In shaping *Half a Look of Cain*, Goyen did not make his alter ego, Chris, the principal narrator of the novel, but preferred to adopt other identities, also, especially that of the attending physical thera-pist and nurse, and then to let Chris speak as if he were another person, who also had his tale to tell. And the nurse, too, who has later become a lighthouse keeper, speaks to the reader only through yet another storyteller who has listened in his time, the unnamed new lighthouse keeper, of whose identity Goyen makes a riddle with one last, surprising clue.

What's always notable in Goyen's fiction is not the possible auto-biographical incident or detail, but rather the unerring instinct with which he could find the emotional meaning and resonance of incident or detail. He did not exactly draw from models in the real-istic manner nor entirely make up what he wrote, but rather, as he said several times, listened to imagined voices who told him their stories, each in his or her own way. He felt that memory and imag-ination worked in him, as if independently of his will and inten-tions, to create the characters he portrayed.

Two and a half years after the letters about his injury, he writes of his work-in-progress to another correspondent on June 5, 1952:

> The tentative title is "Half a Look of Cain" . . . and I
> mean the title to speak about that brotherhood of men
> and women whose faces have in them, as Lawrence said,
> "half a look of gathered love and half a look of Cain." It
> is, then, this work, in a sense, the love story of two young
> people; and it is, too, about a kind of murder where the
> murderers are invisible. The rest lies way down below.

That note of following an instinctual direction in working out, in bringing to light, a novel is very characteristic of Goyen.

Other letters and some working notes from this time show that the core of this novel was always an alertness to, a fictional inquiry into, contradiction and opposition, especially self-contradiction and internal struggle of feelings. The possible plots and stories of the novel changed as Goyen kept writing, till he had constructed this uniquely-shaped novel. But the vision at the center of it remained the same.

In an interview near the end of his life Goyen spoke of revising his work repeatedly but of holding to a central vision of it that remained fixed. Among his papers is a brief undated typewritten document, emended by hand on more than one occasion, that seems to have come out of a moment, perhaps in the midst of revision, when Goyen returned to the vision at the heart of *Half a Look of Cain*. The document is headed with the title of the novel. In the following transcription, handwritten alternatives and additions are set in italics.

> To create a hero; a titanic figure; an old fantastic healer
> or saviour *deliverer* (Curran); the maker, or remaker, arti-
> ficer, fabricateur; he imagines on the grand, heroic, fabu-
> lous (in the sense of <u>fable</u>) scale. The <u>Idea</u> of humanity.

> The idea of collaboration—of Nurse, of healing force,
> and patient, natural force *force of nature* (art). But the
> danger of re-creating <u>against</u> Nature. The danger of <u>the</u>
> <u>idea</u>. Symbol of man on flagpole as the idea <u>above</u> hu-
> manity: does this involvement with a "lofty" idea isolate,
> cut off one from the living world of the ground? Is he
> alienated and desired, too? Mocked, out-cast, yet envied
> and emulated by those below?

> The image of the climber. The rising shape of Shipwreck
> Kelley. The climbing image of the flagpole sitter rising

upwards, escaping upwards to his still place aloft. He was an idea escaping upwards; and the Community both hated him and envied him, adored him and despised him.

A consideration of ancestry, of country, of self, of those loved and betrayed. A purification in the fields of murder (as of Cain) and an atonement for Abel.

Marvello is an outcast of society because he has committed a daring act or gesture which society both fears and envies; he is a hero; he has gone all the way in a personal heroism, in passion.

Man within himself, finding a place within himself to live and endure—*(1)* the tent, *(2)* the Ark-House, etc., *(3)* the lighthouse.

In the form of a journal (The Nurse's) enclosing and founded on a journal or notebook (Chris'). Marvello is the idea created by the "collaboration" of Curren (Nurse) and Christ (the patient). [?] of the creative process. Curran is what Chris will become. Curran—or Charon—is schooling him (Chris), preparing for death, etc. Chris is what Curran was. Marvello is the purified idea of both—their collaborative product.

The crippling in Europe.

The return to Houston—(the rooms in the attic on Austin St. The wide bed. The town [tavern?] lounge across the street from Central High School (Sam Houston High);

Much could be said about these notes on themes, characters, and associations in the novel. That Goyen ended his handwritten additions with a semicolon suggests he was interrupted before he could finish his notes. For our purposes, recovering the novel so many years after it was written, and thinking now about its genesis, it may be enough to see how in Goyen's method of echoes and reiterations of essential dramatic situations, Marvello and other characters accumulate far more symbolic significance than even the author's sketch of his purposes can touch. The reiterated similarities among characters and dramatic situations keep adding layers of meaning to them. Marvello alone has many identities in the book, and from each comes another sense of him as an image of life. Other characters even become Marvello—the flagpole sitter, in his incarnation as the watcher of Chris and Stella, becomes a Marvello, as does Chris in his high observatory of a room after he returns to his hometown, and the new Lighthouse Keeper, himself, in his high lookout, as his last signature attests. With each new instance of this contradictory figure of separateness and observation, loneliness and self-sufficiency, wounding and healing, desiring and being desired, the meaning of Marvello becomes more complex and yet knits to a tighter form, a more intense image.

This is not to imply that the book, for all its resemblance to Goyen's metaphor for his novels—the spatial image of the quilt made of separate medallions—is not also a movement with clear direction. For in working out the progress of the book from tale to tale, Goyen works out stages of feeling and conviction, as well, especially regarding sexuality. The meaning of the order of the incidents in *Half a Look of Cain* might be, in part, that of a progress from the child's seeing of the flagpole sitter, a phallic presence both worshipped and feared, loved and hated; to the young man's experience of the tender attention of the male nurse; and within that moment the experience of his love affair with the young girl, their procreation, their death; then the androgynous or even bisexual image of Marvello, Maria, and Cario, the sexual imagery of their Act; then the final longing for the mirror-image man, the brother-lover, the Cain-and-Abel who meets Chris's long-distance gaze through his own binoculars, and who with Chris tames the wild desire to harm and damage into a tumultuous love. This movement through stages of sexual experience is one of the book's many ideas, or images (that is, neither wholly intellectual nor wholly emotional, but a mixture of both), of human experience. And it is caught in a kind of struggle with itself—that is why the sexual desire of the Chris who is with Stella is so obsessive and insatiable, and that is why the guilty homosexual fantasies and longing of the Chris who seeks out Marvello have made him feel he might as well be a murderer.

It was not likely that such a novel, following the author's deepest intuitions of feeling and his free experiment with form, would produce much enthusiasm in an editor of the day. There was artistic courage in the very writing of this book. When Goyen finished *Half a Look of Cain* he submitted it to Random House, which had published his first two books. To judge from Goyen's letters and from his recollections late in life, his editors seem to have been both admiring and impatient, almost worshipful at some moments, but even then wanting Goyen's next book to be something of a commercial success, as the first two had not been. *Half a Look of Cain* was rejected by Random House; the exasperated Goyen then submitted it to another publishing house, which also rejected it. On May 10,

1953, he wrote to his French translator, Maurice Coindreau, that *Half a Look of Cain*

> is here again, I asked for it back, and I'll think about it a while before letting it go again. . . . The two American publishers who have seen parts of it have for some curious reason been "shocked" by it! This has me bewildered. They all praise the writing, the form, etc., but they profess not to understand what I am talking about!

We cannot know to what extent the editors' professed failure to understand the novel disguised their fear of or distaste for it. Goyen's own letter suggests that they felt, even if they did not admit it openly, that the novel was very much about sexuality, and this was what they were shocked by.

Surprisingly, though, as we can tell from another of Goyen's letters, Coindreau also recommended that Goyen not publish *Half a Look of Cain*. In notes to Goyen's letters Robert Phillips says that "Coindreau had suggested the subject matter of *Half a Look of Cain* was 'ahead of its time,' and publication should be delayed." Again, not (or not only) the novel's structural and narrative experiments but its portrayal of homosexual, as well as heterosexual, desire must account for the inability of an extraordinarily sophisticated reader who was also the translator of Faulkner to have seen the triumph of Goyen's novel. Attitudes prevailed over responsiveness.

In December of that same year, 1953, Goyen wrote to his German translator, Ernst Robert Curtius—one of the greatest humanistic scholars of the age, and also the translator of many twentieth-century works, most famously *The Waste Land* of T. S. Eliot—that *Half a Look of Cain*

> lies in such a buried world—I have lifted the life of it a little; now I let it lie at its own depth—what else? We do have to know what to take, what to turn away from and leave. The life of the work haunts me still, like A Shape of Light that rises from its buried place and goes over the land for a while, bewitching me, then vanishes. But all this says only how I feel about something I have had the audacity to shape among some kind of life, nothing more; only a comment [. . .] I stow away the manuscript and go on to new work.[3]

Robert Phillips says that Curtius, too, "advised Goyen to put *Half a Look of Cain* aside for the time being." Goyen's metaphor of that which lies buried being lifted—into consciousness, into sight—

speaks powerfully of the importance of this book to his understanding of himself as a writer, of his necessary subjects and his artistic project.

But his editors and translators could not see this, nor the value of the book as a response to the America of the 1950s. Yet how can one blame Goyen for submitting to these early judgments and shelving the novel? Reading his letters it is easy, now, to feel on his behalf how heavily these discouragements weighed on him. He believed that he had failed to convey his vision, had failed to realize his work fully. And from time to time he made further revisions in *Half a Look of Cain* (there are at least seven versions of the work in his papers). In 1963, after a last failed attempt to publish it, this time through a new literary agent, Goyen put it aside for the last time. I think this defeat was devastating to him. It took his spirits from him. Not from his own artistic impulse but at another's suggestion, he expanded an earlier story, "The Fair Sister," into a novella, published in 1963; and then was silent. He was forty-eight years old. For a decade, he did not publish any fiction. He wrote for the theater; he worked also as an editor in a commercial publishing house, perhaps trying to extend to other writers the responsiveness that he had not received. These labors and attempts, and his worsening alcoholism, ended his fiction-writing for a time.

His attempts at further revision of *Half a Look of Cain* over the years did not betray the novel for the sake of selling it. Goyen really seems to have been unable to write against himself, to reshape his artistic vision to fit the times. As is immediately apparent now, in the context of all his work, he had not failed his own instincts and purposes in *Half a Look of Cain,* he had only failed to answer to what the age demanded. For he did indeed accomplish a journey, farther than he had gone in *The House of Breath,* into the creation of emblems of feeling, into revelations of the erotic, into the ardent and jealous drama of intimate friendship, and into the powers and formal possibilities of narrative. At considerable cost to himself, Goyen insisted on his formal experiment *and* very deliberately wrote against the fear and apprehension which in most peoples' attitudes surrounded sexuality in the American mid-century—that enforced propriety, that "normalcy" of appearances, while the desires, passions and hopes of the human beings underneath those appearances were as transporting and treacherous as those of any other epoch. From our vantage, indeed, we can see how little Goyen cared for the superficial shocks and pleasures of writing explicitly about sex, and how much he insisted—as most of his contemporaries did not—that erotic life was a profound, formative element of human experience, a primal arena of discovery, transport, struggle, trepidation, bewilderment, danger, need, fulfillment.

Finally, Goyen revived. In 1974 he published his next novel, *Come the Restorer,* and his *Selected Writings,* and in 1975 his *Collected Stories* and a twenty-fifth-anniversary edition of *The House of Breath,* ending the period of silence that had begun when *Half a Look of Cain* was put aside. (Three of his *Collected Stories* were tales from *Half a Look of Cain* that had been published separately.) The truth of his work, which he was unable to abandon even in despair, returned him fully to creativity and productivity in 1976, when he stopped drinking and inaugurated the last period of his writing with the short story "Precious Door." *Half a Look of Cain,* in all its versions, remained among his papers, preserved if not published—a kind of secret lighthouse that his gifts could set their continuing course by, even if no one else knew that such a beacon existed. This last period of his life, till his death in 1983, was as productive as his early years, and marked by great energy and accomplishments, indeed: *Arcadio,* the new stories in his posthumous *Had I a Hundred Mouths,* and other works he left unfinished.

When we feel a writer's importance to us, and we look into the work to find what accounts for this importance, it is often, I think, that the work changes our understanding of what life and writing can be, may be. Because of the emotional intensity and intelligence, the inimitable manner, and the experiments in form in Goyen's fiction, I believe that among American writers of this second half of the century, he has offered us one of the most profound—sometimes wild, sometime delicate—of our opportunities to understand and imagine ourselves.

What is saddening about the case of *Half a Look of Cain* is how vulnerable the writer was to the opinions of those who did not understand what he was doing. How unfortunate it is that readers who were shortly to be offered such defining American novels of the contradictory 1950s as *Invisible Man* and *Catch-22* were not able also to see alongside them another underground current equally strong and equally hidden until it was brought to the surface in Goyen's book. These are all novels of discovery, in the legal sense: bringing to light the evidence of our ways of being. Race rituals; the bleakly, absurdly humorous death and hypocrisy of wartime; and the truth of love and desire, destructiveness and despair: these essential aspects of the American experience were the very 1950s subjects of these novels by Ralph Ellison, Joseph Heller, and William Goyen, novels that lead us into new awareness at the same time they delight us with the play of mind over forms and ideas. Only it turned out that *The House of Breath* had no commercial success and went out of print; and *Half a Look of Cain* was not published in its time.

What is to be celebrated in the case of *Half a Look of Cain* is that the discouragement Goyen suffered did not hurt the book: if anything, it purified it further into just what Goyen wanted it to be. *Half a Look of Cain,* retrieved from Goyen's papers in a research library committed to preserving his work for future readers, now comes to light in an age when it can be seen clearly and its author can speak, from the 1950s, to his true audience of the future. One would think that Goyen's contemporaries could certainly have grasped and appreciated his book if they had had the chance; after all, *The House of Breath* became almost immediately on publication one of the most passionately admired American novels, and has remained so, a book completely unlike any other. But if *Half a Look of Cain* was "ahead of its time," as Coindreau thought, then we are the time it was ahead of. And we can welcome it now.

NOTES

1. The last typescript of *Half a Look of Cain* is dated 1963. This edition is drawn from two lightly hand-corrected photocopies of this typescript, dated 1974, and from additional small changes found in the versions of the three sections which Goyen published as short stories in periodicals and then reprinted in his *Collected Stories* (1975).

2. Goyen's letters, in the manuscript collections of the Harry Ransom Humanities Research Center, are to be published in the fall of 1994 by the University of Texas Press in a volume edited and annotated by Robert Phillips.

3. "A Shape of Light" is one of the stories in *Ghost and Flesh,* a tale told around an elusive nocturnal wisp of light in the East Texas forests, a spirit perhaps.